Rusty Hodgdon

This book is a work of fiction. Names, characters, businesses, organizations, places, events and incidents are products of the author's over-active imagination or are used fictitiously. Any resemblance to actual events, locales or persons, living or dead, is entirely coincidental.

All rights reserved, including the right to reproduce this book or portions thereof in any form whatsoever.

Copyright 2017 by Create Space

Published in the United States by Create Space, a subsidiary of Amazon.com

ACKNOWLEDGEMENTS

Many friends and family assisted me in the writing and editing of this novel. I thank Joyce for her support throughout this process. I also express my great appreciation to the Key West Writers Guild, and especially to Dale Dapkins and Eddie Goldstein, for their excellent input and advice. And many thanks to the Florida Keys Council of the Arts for bestowing upon me the Key West Writers Guild Literary Award.

A Cast of Characters, arranged in order of the chapter and their first appearance, is provided at the end of this novel.

Recipient of the Florida Keys Council of the Arts Key West Writers Guild Literary Award

OTHER NOVELS BY RUSTY HODGDON

THE SUBWAY KILLER

Anthony Johnson is a handsome, charismatic pimp who is suspected of murdering several college co-eds. When Mark Bowden, a young, impressionable Public Defender is assigned to represent him, he quickly finds himself cajoled by the beautiful women of Johnson's stable into going far beyond the bounds of ethical legal conduct.

~SUICIDE

A new arrival to Key West, Dana Hunter only wanted to be left alone to write and enjoy life after raising children and a divorce. But a brief argument in a bar, and the later witnessing of a suicide, lower him into the hellish depths of facing murder charges and police corruption from which only a good lawyer and the love of a woman can resurrect him.

~INSANITY

The denizens of a small town in California start engaging in strange, aberrant behavior. When a young health inspector begins to suspect the cause could be attributed to the spillage of an hallucinogenic chemical into the town's water supply, his efforts to disclose that fact expose him to fatal retribution.

THE PHANTOM WRITER

Ian Anderson is past his prime as a mystery writer. His publisher delivers an ultimatum—take on a ghost writer or we'll drop you. A beautiful, young woman is hired and submits a superlative manuscript. Ian secretly adopts it as his own and finds out the plot describes a real-life crime—with details only the perpetrator would know. How does he explain that?

~THE EYE

A monstrous hurricane forms in Africa, ravages the Cape Verdes, and strikes Bermuda and the Florida coast. Some of the characters believe it is following them in retribution for past sins. Of course, it isn't . . . or is it? This psychological thriller will keep you riveted . . . and squirming.

Chapter One

I'm a lawyer. No, I don't want to hear your favorite lawyer joke. I have my own, thank you. It was a wet blanket June day in Key West, the kind that made you gag as you inhaled. The temp, and the humidity, hovered near ninety. I got a call from Bob. He caught me at home on Waddell Street on a Thursday morning. I never went into the office early on a weekday unless I had to show up in court.

Bob was a good friend, and a client. Which means a non-paying client. We had met years back at the bocce courts over at White and Atlantic. Ended up on the same team—The Green Parrot Gropers. I always thought they had left a "u" out of the name. But then again, this is Key West. I had represented him in some minor criminal matters—mostly driving offenses—nothing of any importance.

He was a kick-ass bocce player. Standing six foot four, he had arms that seemingly extended the length of the court. When he stepped forward, wound up, and let go of the ball, he was almost on top of the "Jack" and other balls at the far end. It gave him a tremendous advantage, and he was the most sought-after player in the league. At just under six feet, and not nearly as athletic, I liked the game because it took neither size nor special ability.

Over the years, Bob had also helped me with some minor jobs around the house. He moved around a lot, and was sometimes hard to find, but when I could track him down, he was a competent, but slow, carpenter

, and a hard worker on more menial tasks. We also met occasionally at the Dog Park off Atlantic Boulevard. His dog, Harley, a Rottweiler-Doberman mutt, and Jessica, my Collie and Shepherd mix, got along well.

"Hey, Sammy, what exactly does a 'person of interest' mean?" Bob asked.

"What?" It was too early in the morning for questions, and I was busy frying two eggs.

"A 'person of interest.' You know, like on TV."

I thought everyone knew what it meant. I liked Bob, but his geese didn't all fly in a straight V. "It means the police have zeroed in on that person for a crime, but probably don't have enough to charge him. Why?"

"Oh, nuthin'."

I knew Bob, and I knew better than that. "C'mon Bob. You wouldn't have called me if it was nothing. Spit it out."

There was a lengthy pause. "Okay. The police stopped by my home last night. Asked me a lot of questions."

"And?"

"That's all."

This was quickly becoming tedious. "Questions about what, for Christ's sake?"

"Did you hear about that young girl they found? Over in the mangroves by the Salt Ponds?"

Selfie

I knew the Salt Ponds were located across from South Roosevelt Boulevard and Smathers Beach on the Atlantic Ocean side of Key West. They got their name because salt was harvested from them over a century ago. There was also a Bridle Path—a sandy, unpaved road lined with palm trees—between the Boulevard and the Ponds that had been used as a trail for riding horses some fifty plus years ago. Still retained the name. Thick stands of mangroves separated the Ponds from the Bridle Path.

"Yeah," I said. "Right next to the Bridle Path. Was in today's *Citizen*. Body was discovered the day before yesterday—in the evening. Terrible. First murder in the Keys this year. But why were they questioning you?"

"Bridal Path? I didn't know they did weddings over there. I've only seen them on Smathers."

I let out a long sigh. "No, Bob. Bridle Path. B . . . R . . . I . . . D . . . L . . . E Path. Like for horses."

"Oh .I got it. Well, I was there that day, walking Harley. Someone I knew was driving down Roosevelt and waved to me. Guess they told the cops. The two guys who paid me a visit said they were just following up on all leads, but by the end of our conversation I was sure they thought I was involved. When they left, they told me I was a person of interest and that I should stay in town for a while."

I was pissed now. "Jesus, Bob. You spoke to the cops without calling me first? I've told you several times never to do that."

"Take it easy, Sam. I didn't know why they showed up on my

doorstep. By the time I did know, there was no time to call 'ya. Am I in some kinda' trouble, d'ya think?"

I sensed a tinge of panic in his voice, so I said, "Not if you didn't have anything to do with it, which I know you didn't. Look, do not, under any circumstances, speak to anyone about this except me. If it's the cops, tell 'em you've got a lawyer, and give them my name and telephone number. They can't ask you any questions then. I'll be willing to take a call or two from them if necessary."

"Okay, I'll do it. But where do we go from here?"

I didn't like the word "we" in this context. Especially from Bob. It surely meant another freebie was on the way. "Tell you what. I'll poke around a little bit. See what I can find out. I'll let you know."

"Gosh, Sam. I appreciate that. I'll never be able to repay you."

Truer words were never spoken.

Chapter Two

It was time for my Friday night rendezvous with Janine. I had met her at the Green Parrot a year and a half ago. She had grown up in San Francisco and at age twenty-five traveled to Key West for a one week vacation. She never left. We call it a staycation down here. Happens a lot. I had been to Frisco twice in my life—once on a cross-county, Route 66-style trip in a new Camaro I had bought during the summer after my sophomore year in college—then six years later for a job interview in my last year in law school. I liked the ambiance of the City, and I immediately perceived certain similarities between the two towns when I moved to Key West. Both exuded a spirit of acceptance and carefreeness.

My experience with the California ladies was they considered sensuality to be a natural by-product of living. I got laid more times in those several days in Frisco than any comparable period in my life. The girls said they liked my surfer look—I was blessed, or maybe cursed, with natural sandy blond hair, green eyes and a complexion that tanned well.

Janine Williams confirmed these initial impressions. She broadcast sexuality. Not exactly pretty, yet well put together—5'1", generously buxom, with a prominent nose and impeccable dark complexion. That first night we went back to my place and did everything—all positions, and the best blow job ever, with a very happy ending.

I would have liked to see her more often, but she was in control. She worked as a private massage therapist, and was very much in demand. I got my free massage once a week. So, it was every Friday for dinner at the Grand, one of the better eateries in town, right on Duval Street, and then escapades after. She always quietly slithered out of my bed sometime in the wee morning hours.

When we were seated for dinner, I told her about my conversation with Bob. I was surprised to find she knew him. I didn't push the issue further. She was pleased I had agreed to help him out. We had a great meal and enjoyed dessert at home.

Over the next several weeks I ran into the two detectives—Kenneth Phillips and Robert Albury—who had interviewed Bob. I had known them on and off over the ten years I'd been practicing law in town.

****

I came down to Key West from Chicago back then on a whim. A friend who had been here called it the end of the earth, and there was something in my composition that liked that. I visited during my one-week vacation from the big law firm job I had nabbed immediately after law school. Fell in love with the place. I only lasted six more months at that job, and hated every ticking moment of it. My windowless cubicle, where I was expected to toil alone ten to twelve hours a day, six days a week, was eight by eight feet square.

All that with the fragile expectation I'd make partner in seven years.

About fifty per cent lasted that distance, and only a third of those acquired partnership. Didn't like those odds. I packed up Jessica, some shorts, T-shirts, flip-flops, and just enough work clothes to get by, and drove down. As the song says, "Sell the stuff, keep the dog, and move to an island."

Very soon, I sold my BMW 300i and purchased a used Jeep Wrangler. Its soft top had long since evaporated, and the few times it rained, I wore my poncho. But Key West is a biking town, so my most valued asset is my Trek twenty-one speed. There's only one hill in town—we call it Solares Hill—and it's eighteen feet above sea level. I learned to bike everywhere, reserving the car for occasional food shopping trips and my rare forays to the Upper Keys. I loved the freedom of the openness of the bike and the no-hassle parking. A new back pack supplanted my former, patent leather legal briefcase.

I had the reserves to buy a small house—they call them "conch" houses down here. Hundreds were built in the late 1800s and early 1900s to shelter the thousands of cigar manufacturing workers who emigrated here from Cuba and South America. Mine sat on a postage stamp lot of just five thousand square feet. You entered the front door into a small anteroom, which I used as my living room, then proceeded down a long hallway, giving access to the three tiny bedrooms. At the end was the kitchen, the largest room in the house, with the lone bathroom to the left. I took most of my showers in the enclosed outdoor shower—heck, it rarely got below fifty-five degrees here. My landscaping consisted of a tangle of small palms, frangipani, and sea grass. Low maintenance, low cost.

****

The cops were tight-lipped as usual, but suggested to me that Bob was not as forthcoming as they would expect from an innocent man. I let them know I was representing him—at least for purposes of the investigation—and would be glad to meet with them, alone, to explain why it was impossible for the Bob I knew to have been involved. They appeared completely disinterested. I thought the matter was done with.

Imagine my surprise when I read in the Crime Report of the *Key West Citizen* four weeks later that Bob had been arrested for the first-degree murder of thirteen-year-old Frances Lathrop, the girl whose body was found off the Bridle Path. A few calls later, I was at the county jail on Stock Island where Bob was being held.

I met him in the attorney's area, a section of the regular visitation room separated by carpeted dividers. It contained a small desk and two folding chairs. I had been there many times before.

I could hardly believe it was Bob who came into the enclosure. He had a large bandage around his head, his eyes were a dark red-purplish color, and his bloated lower lip hung almost to his chin.

"What the fuck happened to you?" I said, before he had a chance to sit down.

Bob was a big boy, and he filled the entrance. I knew him as a gentle giant, but he also reminded me of what nuclear deterrence meant—there was always an underlying feeling he could explode like an "H" bomb at any time. Nobody fooled with him.

"Oh," as if he was surprised I asked. "I didn't know it was the cops who came through my front door. It was two other plainclothes detectives. Didn't recognize them. I thought they were going to rob me. Guess they didn't appreciate me throwing my bar stool at them."

"You threw a bar stool at the cops? What the hell's the matter with you?"

A slyness formed on his distorted lips. "I didn't know who they were."

"Okay. Okay. I bet they're going to add charges of assault and battery on a law enforcement officer as well as resisting arrest. Not that it matters with the homicide charge."

Bob sat down on the only other folding metal chair in the room, turning its back toward me and straddling the opposite side. "What evidence do they have?" he asked.

"I don't really know. Won't find out for a while. But I haven't agreed to formally represent you now that charges have been brought. You're probably eligible for a public defender. I work for money now. And I know you don't have the kind of cash I would charge."

"C'mon, Sam. Can't you ask the court to appoint you to represent me, oh what do they call it, on a pro-bone basis?"

"It's *pro bono* Bob," but even his bastardization of the term alerted me to the fact that Bob knew more about the judicial system than I had imagined. "I stopped doing that work years ago."

"I don't mean for free. If they're going to pay a public defender, why can't they pay you? I know you and trust you. You won that last murder case you handled."

I knew of what he spoke. Shortly after my arrival in Key West I was retained by a man charged with first degree murder. It was my first one and I would either make a big splash in the legal arena if I won it, or have to flee with my tail between my legs if I lost. That's because it was a case that was winnable. Not all are.

There was no question that my guy had shot the victim. The only issue was whether he acted in self-defense. Fernando, my client, had struck up an affair with a married, but separated woman. She lived in the home, and the husband, a wife-abuser and first-class louse, was restrained from coming into the house.

That didn't deter this lunatic spouse. Somehow, he convinced a professional photographer to come with him in a stealth mission to catch her in bed with my client. Apparently, he held the demented opinion that such evidence would help him in the divorce.

The husband decided he would be safer if he brought a Louisville Slugger with him. So, into the house they go at two a.m., the husband using a spare set of keys. As they entered the bedroom, the photographer began clicking away, the flash illuminating the scene. What the victim didn't anticipate was that my client had a legal .38 under his pillow.

My client awoke from the noise and light, saw the baseball bat, and fired six shots into the husband. The photographer turned tail and made it out alive.

After I laid out in detail to the jury what a total scumbag the victim was, and the judge instructed them on the "stand your ground" defense that is still controversial in Florida, the courtroom gallery erupted in applause upon the not guilty verdict. And something happened I had never witnessed before—half the jury also clapped, and many came down to give my guy a pat on the back. That one case alone was worth thousands of dollars in advertising.

I didn't want to get involved with Bob's case. I mean, I liked Bob and all, but how well did I really know him? Or anyone for that matter? I'd been lied to by the best, and found out the hard way not to place too much trust in what people accused of a crime told me. "I'll see what I can do," I said, fully expecting to do nothing.

I turned to go when Bob said, some panic in his voice, "Sammy, Harley's been cooped up for over sixteen hours now. Can you keep him for a while, at least until we clear this up?"

I couldn't say no. Jessie and Harley were best buds and I didn't want to be stuck cleaning up the mess. "Sure."

I picked up Harley at Bob's house. Bob never locked his door. Harley eyed me suspiciously from the couch as I entered, then recognized me and jumped down and began licking my hand furiously. I let him out the back door to the yard. He lifted his leg just down the stairs and emptied his bladder for a full, solid minute. I won't mention the other, but I had to use the wheelbarrow to clean it up.

Jessica was ecstatic. She had a play friend to occupy her normally isolated existence. For the first month, Harley sat expectantly just inside the door, waiting for Bob. After a while, he settled into our daily routine and spent most of the time on the large doggy bed I purchased for him that I placed next to Jessie's. There they would often lie, their noses no more than two inches apart, waiting for me to take them out.

Each morning I would escort them to Dog Park off Atlantic Avenue. It's divided into big and small dog sections. Harley was in a large area, and Jessica insisted on being there as well with her friend. I had always placed her with the lesser sized canines for fear of her being hurt by the assortment of Mastiffs, German Shepherds, Dobermans and Pit Bulls that dominated the larger dog population. Harley was well-behaved and docile despite his fearsome mien, just like his daddy. Once, however, he did grab a frisky Great Dane, who had played too rough with him, by the throat and held him down on the ground for a minute to teach him a lesson. No dog bothered him, or Jessica, after that.

On special occasions, I would take them to the beach. There's a "dog beach" in Key West, right next to Louie's Backyard, a popular locals' hang-out, where dogs can run free on the beach and in the ocean. They were both excellent swimmers, and loved it. I couldn't bear to take them to the Bridle Path. I don't believe in ghosts but I had a hard time ridding myself of the image of Frances, bloodied and mud-encrusted, clawing her way out of the Salt Pond toward me. It also reminded me of the fact that Bob might never get home to be with his beloved Harley.

Damn my luck. A day after my meeting with Bob I got a call from Judge Jeremiah Thorpe. The best judge on the bench in Key West, in my opinion. A no-nonsense guy.

"Attorney Harris, I have a letter here in front of me from an inmate over there at the County jail named Bob Wilson." Judge Thorpe's vocal resonance was as impressive over the phone as it was in person. "He wants you to represent him. He's charged with murder. I contacted the Public Defenders Office and they told me they have a conflict of interest in representing him."

"Why's that?" I asked.

"One of the attorneys in their office represented Wilson on charges of disturbing the peace and possession of marijuana three years previously. Wilson filed a complaint against that attorney with the Florida Bar. It's still pending. They feel no one in the office can represent him until that's resolved."

My throat began constricting to the point where I could barely breathe. I knew where this was going.

"I agree with them," the Judge continued. "So, I'm appointing you."

I couldn't speak. It was a huge mistake for me to get involved in Bob's case. We were too close. I also didn't want to work for the pittance the State paid court-appointed lawyers. But this was JudgeThorpe. Calling me personally.

"Attorney Harris. Are you still there?"

I rasped, "Judge I'm honored, but I'm not capital case certified." I knew that to be appointed, as opposed to being privately retained, to a murder case in Florida, you had to have a certain level of experience in felony cases and be certified by the Florida Supreme Court.

"I've taken care of that. Justice Wharton on the Court is a good friend of mine from Stanford Law School. We reviewed your experience and record and your certification is already in the mail."

"Um . . . okay, judge. Then I'd be honored to accept the appointment."

Man, was I pissed. I picked up my written appointment at the clerk's office and checked the docket entries. Dan Thompson was prosecuting the case. I knew Dan. A real pain in the ass. Every case he handled was just another notch in his gun grip that would lead him to the State House in Tallahassee. He was ridiculously hardline and always looked for the maximum sentence allowable regardless of the circumstances. He wouldn't lose any votes doing that.

The good news was he was a pretty boy in a stuffed suit, having barely made it through law school and flunking the bar exam three times before miraculously passing on his fourth try. There was a rumor circulating around that he paid someone to take the last exam for him.

I headed straight to his office in the courthouse complex on Whitehead Street. I was surprised to find him there rather than at the Green Parrot where he regularly took lengthy liquid lunches. As usual, I saw him at his desk through a large plate-glass window, just catty-corner from the receptionist. I walked right past Cheri, his gate keeper, and into his office. He looked like the consummate politician—meticulously attired, hair coiffed to perfection and a tanned face that I heard came from a salon, not the nearby beaches.

"Hey, Sam. What can I do for you?" He remained seated and continued to stare at a computer screen, which because it was slightly turned my way, revealed an array of photographs of what looked like scantily-clad high school cheerleaders. And they picked this guy to lead the attack against a purported killer of a young girl? Give me a break.

"Oh, hi, Dan. Didn't expect to find you in. Thought you'd be out catchin' criminals."

"I don't catch 'em. I put 'em away," he snarled back.

"Ah, so you do."

"Anything I can do for you?" Clearly irritated now.

"I understand you've got the Bob Wilson case. I've been appointed to represent him."

"I heard. Sure you're up to it?"

I refused to show *my* irritation. "No problem. Should be easy. There's no credible evidence against him."

"Don't jump to any premature conclusions, Attorney Harris. In fact, you're lucky we can't seek the death penalty against this child killer."

I knew what he was referring to. The United States Supreme Court had recently ruled that Florida's death penalty was unconstitutional. The state had tried in earnest to pass an acceptable death statute, but had woefully failed. No one would lose a penny underestimating the collective stupidity of the Florida Legislature.

"Okay, Dan, why don't we just dispense with the formalities of the discovery process? Give me everything you got right now," and I began to open my briefcase. I knew there was no chance Dan would agree to bypass the procedural rules of discovery.

"Nice try, Attorney Harris. File your motions, and I'll respond." He resumed staring at his computer.

I couldn't help myself. "I hope there are no shots of Frances Lathrop among that bunch." I quickly strode out of the office, not once looking back to see the outrage I knew would be on his face.

Chapter Three

I filed my motions. Perfunctory, because there was a mandatory discovery rule that required both the prosecution and defense to reveal what evidence they had. Necessary, because I anticipated Dan Thompson's stonewalling everything I sought to find out.

I next submitted paperwork to reduce Bob's bail, which had been set at a million dollar's cash. With the seriousness of the charges, Bob's prior record—even though minor, and his peripatetic nature, I estimated the chances of accomplishing the mission were slim. But I had to try.

I also visited him again at the jail. I had nothing of an evidentiary nature to raise his spirits, but I knew from experience anyone in his shoes relished breaks in the monotony of their prison existence. I respected him for his bravado under the circumstances. Not once did he complain or blame me for his predicament—a rare occurrence indeed.

I did explore in detail everything Bob had done in the days of and surrounding the killing of Frances. The day before the discovery of the body, he went to work at Strunk Hardware and left at five, a fact I confirmed with his boss. Then he went to Turtle Kraals for oysters and conch chowder and left at nine to return home. Charlie, the bartender, remembered him and how long he stayed.

Bob told me he had gotten up around 8 a.m. on the day Frances was found. As he did every morning, he immediately took Harley out for a walk on the Bridle Path. As he explained to me, "Sammy, you don't make a dog of Harley's pedigree and size wait too long to shit and pee. One time I was outrageously hungover and wouldn't get up. He ripped the pillow, sheets and blanket off the bed and finally grabbed my T-shirt by the sleeve and pulled me onto the floor."

Bob lived in a studio apartment on Leon Street, just around the corner from Bertha and South Roosevelt Boulevard. It was only a ten-minute walk to the Bridle Path. There, he was afforded a carefree, dog-off-leash promenade to the airport and back, a distance of almost a mile each way. He stopped as he usually did at an opening in the foliage and threw sticks into the Salt Ponds for Harley to retrieve. He saw nothing out of the ordinary.

It was his day off so he performed some odd jobs around his place, then hung at the Raw Bar over lunchtime. Again, Val, one of the barkeeps, attested to his presence. He returned home, and around 4:00 p.m. took Harley for his late afternoon walk on the Path. He stayed home all night and watched Ground Hog Day, his favorite movie. "Had watched it twenty-two times," he told me. He did recall hearing someone honk at him that afternoon as he was walking Harley, but didn't see who it was.

"I was surprised anyone was hurt there around that time," he added. "There was a police cruiser parked on the Bridle Path for a few minutes while I was there."

"The cops were there? What time?"

Selfie

"I don't really remember, but it was while I was walking Harley."

"That's interesting," I said.

After our interview at the jail, I went to the spot off the Bridle Path he had described. It afforded one of the few clear openings to the Ponds. I walked to the edge of the water—there were the remnants of an old pier extending a few feet out into the water. Several chunks of coral rock spotted the area. Stout pieces of wood of various sizes, evidently from the pier, lay scattered about.

Bob's version of events sounded simple and plausible—until I got the police and forensic reports two days later. I read them at home with growing trepidation. The Crime Scene Report, signed by the two uniforms, Officers Butler and Murphy, who were first called to the location, contained these passages:

Officer Butler and I arrived at the Salt Ponds at 6:25 p.m. on June 14. We had been dispatched pursuant to a 911 emergency call to central. We were first met by Ms. Lisa Mallory who had made the call. She directed us to an area near the Salt Ponds immediately opposite to the break in the sea wall at the easterly end of Smathers Beach. There was a dilapidated pier that extended approximately ten feet out into the Ponds. At the base of the pier we found the body of a young girl, age estimated to be in her early teens. She was lying on her side, poised in a fetal position. Her feet were partially in the water. She was wearing light tan shorts and a dark blue shirt. We determined her to be deceased. It appeared she had blunt force trauma wounds to the head.

A search of the area around the body disclosed a red Schwinn, single speed girls bicycle, laying on its side near the pond, and several 2x2 square inch pieces of wood—two feet long, probably oak and braces from the pier. One specifically attracted our attention—it had a vague maroon stain on the upper portion and what appeared to be two strands of hair embedded in the grain of the wood. The pieces were bagged and the Crime Scene Emergency Response Team was called. There was no sign of a struggle in the immediate area so our first impression was that the body may have been brought to the location, dumped, and then beaten with the club.

Detectives Philips and Albury each wrote lengthy reports. Detective Albury's was the most damaging. It read, in part:

Detective Phillips and I arrived unannounced at Robert Wilson's home at 1102 Leon Street at ten o'clock p.m. on June 15. It did not appear he was surprised to see us. We informed him we were investigating the death of Frances Lathrop on June 14. He invited us into his apartment, consisting of one room with a small kitchenette. We read him his full Miranda rights, which he said he understood. He admitted he was in the area on the day when Miss Lathrop's body was found. Mr. Wilson said he was walking his dog. He was evasive about the time and how long he was there. Both Detective Phillips and I felt he was not fully forthcoming about his activities. At the end of our interview we asked him if he'd be willing to undergo a polygraph examination and he said he'd have to speak with an attorney before agreeing to that. His response was the same when we asked him for a DNA sample.

****

A thin smile crept over my lips. I distinctly remembered the

Selfie

conversation. A couple of months prior, Bob and I were having drinks at Schooner Wharf Bar and Grille over at the Seaport in the early afternoon. Michael McCloud, a stalwart of the afternoon Schooner's crowd for over twenty years, was playing his eclectic mix of covers and originals. As it often did, the subject matter turned to the law. Bob enjoyed hearing my war stories. He had interrupted me to talk about an episode of *Identification Discovery,* also known as "ID," his favorite TV show.

"So, yeah, the cops had this perp in the interrogation room. He had been in there for about three hours. He had denied everything up to that point. For some reason, he agreed to take a polygraph. I happen to think he convinced himself he hadn't done the crime. They administered the polygraph in another room. The perp had a smirk on his face the whole time. Very street-wise. Then they let him cool his jets in interrogation for another hour.

"When they came back in, they leaned on him hard. Even brought the lie detector guy in. They were screaming at him, telling him he had flunked the test hands-down. Within a half-hour, he gave it all up—even admitted to a prior murder. He was bawling at the end. Sammy, why would anyone who was guilty agree to a lie detector test in the first place? Do you have to take one if they demand it?"

I took a sip of my Bud Light Lime. I could see a long answer forthcoming. "As to your first question, I think it's because people wrongly believe they'll be arrested if they refuse it. On the second one, the short answer is 'no.' The general public doesn't realize it, but polygraphs are one step below tea leaf reading. They're total bullshit. The cops use it to extract confessions"

Bob shifted in his chair. "That's not what I've heard. I thought courts allowed the results as evidence."

"Not anymore."

****

I continued reading. There was this report from Detective Phillips:

After our interview with Mr. Wilson, and based on our suspicions he was hiding something from us, we took turns following him over the next several days. One of our purposes was to secretly obtain a DNA sample from him. We also wanted to obtain a DNA sample from his dog. We had an easier time with the dog, identified as "Harley." Harley dropped one of his many yard toys, a section of thick rope with rawhide ends, near the fence to Mr. Wilson's property. We reached it through the chain link.

Mr. Wilson was more difficult. Following him was like taking a bar stroll through the entire town. The first night he hit five establishments. He always carried around the same insulated mug and did not dispose of anything that might bear his DNA. Finally, on June 18, at the 801 Bourbon, he bought a drink in a red plastic cup and left it on the stage in front of where he was seated. We were forced to wait there for three hours before retrieving it from the establishment.

My reading was rudely interrupted by a loud knocking on the screen door. I was so startled I dropped the packet of reports that had been on my lap. I looked up and saw a man—at least 6'3" and in his late thirties—standing on my porch. His distraught, angry look frightened me. I stood up and moved closer to the entrance to my kitchen at the back of the house and said in a shaky voice, "Can I help you?"

"Are you Sam Harris?" he replied gruffly.

"Who's asking?" I decided I could play tough too, even though I was all too conscious my knees were quivering. He opened the screen door and stepped inside.

"You come one step closer and I'm calling the police." I patted my pocket for my phone, only then realizing it was sitting on the kitchen counter a good fifteen feet away.

"Be my guest, asshole. You're representing that dirt-bag Wilson, aren't you?"

"Yes, I've been appointed to represent him. Who are you?" It was at that point I first noticed his short-cropped, ruddy hair.

"Jerry Lathrop. And I'm your worst fuckin' nightmare."

Now things came into focus. This man was thirteen-year-old Frances Lathrop's father. "But . . ." I stammered.

"Shut up," he screamed. He pulled a gun from his waistband. It looked like a police-issue Glock.

"Now Mr. Lathrop, there's no need for this . . ."

He thrust the palm of his free hand in front of my face and gently placed the weapon on the small table near my front door. He reached into his left trouser pocket and pulled out three bullets and a clip. Expertly inserting one bullet into the clip he said, "If that fucker

Wilson is found not guilty, this first one's for him." Pushing the second bullet in, he continued, "This second one's for you." The third bullet went in. "And this last one's for me. Got the message?"

I nodded my head up and down, a little feverishly I suspect. He shoved the loaded clip back into his pocket and the Glock in his waistband, turned and walked out the door, slamming the wooden frame harshly in the process. Just outside, he turned and with a venomous grin said through the screen, "Now go ahead and call the cops."

I waited for him to get to the street before doing so. I told the female dispatcher a man had entered my home without permission and threatened me. When asked if I knew who it was I said, "The father of that young girl who was murdered at the Salt Ponds a few weeks ago."

There was an eerie pause on the line. When I questioned whether she was still there, the lady said, "I'll send someone right out."

I waited a good fifteen minutes, looking out the door every minute or so. Was this the typical emergency response time? I had never had to call 911 in Key West. I called again. The same dispatcher answered. I didn't need to say anything.

"Mr. Harris," she said with irritation in her voice. "They're on their way. Please don't call again." The phone went dead.

A full ten minutes later a cop car pulled up front and I went out to greet them. The two cops who exited motioned me back into the house.

When they entered, the shorter but very stocky one, said, "So we hear you gave Officer Lathrop a hard time."

Selfie

"What?" I could barely speak. My first thought was that two imposters had entered my home.

"Yeah, Officer Lathrop said he stopped by to speak with you about the Harris case, and you were very belligerent. Ordered him out of your house."

"What do you mean by 'officer?' Is he a cop?"

"Yep. Fifteen years on the force. Has been out on leave for the past year."

"Well, you heard wrong. He came inside without permission and threatened my client and myself with a gun. That's what really happened."

The taller one said, with a look of bemusement on his face, "Oh, we don't think so. We know Officer Lathrop well. He would never threaten anyone."

"Well, I'd still like you to write a report on what happened."

"You can come down to the station and talk to Chief Fitzpatrick if you want. But I wouldn't advise it. The Chief's very pissed off about his friend's daughter. Not sure he'd be too friendly with the attorney who's representing the murderer. We suggest you drop the whole thing."

I had been a criminal defense attorney long enough to know when it was time to retreat and regroup to fight another day. "You're right. I'll do just that."

Chapter Four

I needed a drink. I went to my kitchen, poured a shot of American Honey Whiskey, downed one, then another. Feeling better, I returned to my perusal of the investigative reports. There was a packet of ten 8" x 10" photographs, all glossy color. They were unremarkable, only showing in redundancy the crime scene from various angles. Sure enough, there was also the obligatory autopsy report from the State Medical Examiner:

Summary Autopsy Report

Date and Hour Autopsy Performed: June 15, 2016, 8:30 AM	Case #: 001294-33E-2016
Autopsy performed by Manish Awagar. M.D. 1030 N. Roosevelt Blvd Unit 406 Key West FL 33040	Assistant: Victoria White, M.D.
Name: Frances P. Lathrop	Coroner's Case #: 2016-11
Date of Birth: 11/18/2002	Age: 13
Date of Death:	Investigative Agency:

| June 14, 2016 | Key West Police Department. |
| | Monroe County Sherriff's Office. |

External Examination:

The autopsy is begun at 8:30 A.M. on June 15, 2016.

The body is presented in a black body bag. The victim is wearing a blue sleeveless crewneck shirt and khaki shorts. The clothing is torn at places and stained with mud and sand particles. Jewelry included two smooth-textured, silver-hoop pierced earrings, one-half inch diameter, one in each ear, and a one- inch-wide silver expandable wristband on the left wrist.

The body is that of a normally developed white female child measuring 62 inches and weighing 90 pounds, and appearing generally consistent with the stated age of thirteen years. The body is cold and unembalmed. Lividity is fixed in the distal portions of the limbs. The eyes are open. The irises are green and corneas are cloudy. The pupils measure 0.3 cm. The hair is red, wavy, and approximately 11 inches in length at the longest point. Blood-stained froth is found around the mouth and nostrils.

Multiple ligature marks and continuous and horizontal bruises with nail scratch abrasions were found on both sides of the neck, more towards the nape of the neck. The hyoid bone is fractured.

There is evidence of blunt force trauma to the head.

I knew a fracture of the hyoid bone indicated the child had been strangled.

The Report was accompanied by a separate set of photographs of Frances. I didn't want to look at them, but had to. Thank God they were black and white, and not color. The skull was clearly cracked and indented in the left temple area, revealing the trauma caused by some blunt object.

The Report continued in its **Internal Examination**:

Genital Findings:
Bruises on the labia minora, recent hymnal tears at 5 and 7 o'clock position with oozing of blood and a tear of the posterior fourchette.
Anal Findings:
Two small linear abrasions extending from anal margin into the anus with dilatation (3.5x2 cm size) and a bruise at its right margin with laceration of size (1.5x0.5 cm) and fissure was seen around the anus.

I started to shake uncontrollably, and I dropped the report. This poor girl had not only been strangled and bludgeoned, but also raped, both vaginally and anally. What kind of monster would do that?

I skimmed the report to see if any sperm was found in or on the victim. It was not. That meant the perpetrator had to be wearing a condom, which in turn meant he was most likely prepared for the assault.

Then the clincher—the report from the Florida State

Laboratory. These were the pertinent sections:

"*Various items, including tissue and blood samples, were received from The Florida State Police. These were labeled* **Exhibits 2016-20-0001** *through* **2016-20-0017.**

"**Exhibit 2016-20-0001:** *a tissue sample reportedly taken from the body of the decedent, Frances Lathrop.*"

I skimmed quickly over Exhibits 0002 through 00013 because they were items of clothing worn by the victim, some jewelry, and random pieces of flora removed from the scene. Frances' shorts were labelled Exhibit 00013. The others were of little consequence to me at this time.

I continued reading:

"**Exhibit 2016-20-00014:** *a piece of rope, approximately ½ in diameter, with rawhide stitched into the ends.*"

"**Exhibit 2016-20-00015:** *a red plastic cup.*"

I realized these were the items the cops retrieved to obtain DNA samples from Harley and Bob.

"**Exhibit 2016-20-00016:** *a piece of wood, oak, twenty-nine inches long and approximately two-inches square. There were blood stains, several strands of hair, and tissue clearly evident on the surface of the wood.*"

That had to be the murder weapon, I thought.

"**Exhibit 2016-20-00017:** *a piece of wood, twenty inches long and two inches square, similar in appearance and material to Exhibit 2015-20-00016. There was no discernible blood, tissue or hairs on this exhibit. It did contain what appeared to be recent puncture marks in the relative middle of the exhibit.*"

This Exhibit was clearly the stick of wood Bob had told me he was throwing into the water for Harley to retrieve.

"A DNA profile was developed from Exhibit 0001, the tissue from the decedent. Exhibits 00014 through 00017 were swabbed and DNA profiles were developed from those swabs. Our conclusions are as follows:

1. *The DNA developed from the hair and blood on Exhibit 00016 were an exact match of the DNA of the victim.*
2. *Canine DNA was found on Exhibit 00014, the piece of rope. That DNA was also found on Exhibit 00017.*
3. *The human DNA found on Exhibit 00015, the plastic cup, was also found on Exhibits 00016 and 00017. (It should be noted that the human DNA on Exhibit 00016 that matched the DNA from the red cup was trace DNA).*
4. *Exhibit 00017 also contained the DNA of an unknown human, probably male."*
5. *Exhibit 00013 contained the victim's DNA, and the DNA from an unknown donor, also probably male.*

Christ. This was looking bad. Bob's DNA was on the murder weapon. My mind raced . . . in reverse mode. A hundred thoughts of good times with Bob flashed through my brain. Were they all phony? Was this very decent, lovable goofball a child rapist and killer? I couldn't conceive of it. But the facts seemed to point in another direction. I also wondered what that unknown donor DNA was, and was it from the same person?

Selfie

I called Dan and felt fortunate to find him in the office. I asked him if they had run the unknown donor DNA through Codis, the Combined DNA Index System. He said they had, and there were no hits.

I had to speak to Bob again. That opportunity came when I was called by the Clerk's office to tell me my motion to reduce Bob's bail had been scheduled for the next day. Thanks for the ample time to prepare for it. It was too late to visit Bob in jail that afternoon, so I arrived early the next morning at the courthouse to meet with him downstairs in the lockup.

He was brought in late, around 9:30, with court supposed to commence at 10:00 sharp. Bob was garbed in the standard prison issue, almost comical black stripes on orange background. It looked two sizes too small for him. I went briefly over his background, which with his one-parent upbringing, six-month drop-out status from college, and minor criminal record, was not helpful.

They brought him up as court was starting. He sat, shackled, off to the left in the jury box with some other defendants whose cases were being heard that day. Our case was the third to be called. Even though it was our motion, and therefore I should have been the first to address the court, Dan Thompson rose and started to talk over me as I began to present my case. I would have none of it. I raised my voice by fifty decibels, prompting Judge Thorpe to slam his gavel harshly on the hardwood bench.

"Attorneys Harris and Thompson. Enough!" he boomed. "Sit down Mr. Thompson. Now, Attorney Harris, proceed."

I smirked as Dan slunk to his chair.

"Thank you, Your Honor. First, I'm requesting a continuance of the hearing on this motion so I can better prepare for it. I was notified of this hearing just yesterday . . ."

"There will be no continuance, Attorney Harris," the judge interrupted. "I've read the police reports attached to the prosecution's brief in opposition to your motion . . ."

Now it was my turn to cut in. "Brief, Your Honor? I never received a brief from Mr. Thompson."

Judge Thorpe pushed his glasses lower on his nose and peered down at Thompson. "Mr. Thompson, did you not serve Mr. Harris with a copy of your brief?"

Dan stuttered, "Of . . . of course we did, Judge. Mailed it yesterday."

"Isn't Attorney Harris' office just around the corner from yours, on Fleming Street?"

I could tell Dan knew where this was going. "I believe it is, but Judge, I can't hand deliver every notice I send out."

"Well, Mr. Thompson, you certainly should have done just that in this case." Judge Thorpe exhaled in disgust, then turned his attention to me. "But Mr. Harris, is it safe to assume you've received copies of all the police and investigative reports in this case?"

"I've received some, Your Honor, but I don't know if they're *all* of the reports."

The Judge went through the dates and authors of the various

reports attached to Dan's brief, and I had to acknowledge I'd received them.

"I'm very disappointed in the prosecutor for not insuring you received his brief before this hearing," he continued, "but I'm satisfied you've seen the meat of his submission. And based on these reports, I think there is probable cause to conclude Mr. Wilson committed this crime. Also, based on Mr. Wilson's criminal history and sporadic work record, I deem him to be a sufficient flight risk to deny your motion to reduce bail, with the proviso that you can bring it back before me if any new evidence comes forth that might tend to exonerate Mr. Wilson." Another sharp report from his gavel. Out of the corner of my eye, I saw Thompson grinning.

But Judge Thorpe continued. "Mr. Harris, I assume you'll want to hire your own experts to try to rebut the State's scientific conclusions, isn't that right?"

Now it was my turn to beam. It was rare for a judge to raise this issue without a specific written request by the defense. "Yes, Your Honor," I answered, a bit too enthusiastically.

"I'm ruling, *sua sponte*, that Mr. Harris has a right to such experts, and I'm authorizing up to twenty thousand dollars for him to do so."

That was a huge amount to order the State of Florida to pay, and Dan immediately rose to protest.

"Sit back down, Mr. Thompson. That's my ruling. Now the court will take a brief recess."

With that, Judge Thorpe exited through the door behind the

dais.

They quickly escorted Bob back to the lock-up. He was distraught, even though I had made it clear to him that bail was a near impossibility in a capital murder case. I spoke with him through the bars of the small holding cell.

"So, Sam, you mean I have to stay in jail until my trial? How long will that be?"

"Until, as the judge said, new facts come out that show you're not guilty. Remember, Bob, this is a murder case. It will be at least . . ."

"Like a few weeks?" Bob interrupted. "Most of the crime shows on TV have the guy in court in no time. You can do that, can't you?"

TV lawyer shows were the bane of my profession. Everyone thought a criminal case could be brought to trial in a few months, if not weeks, and the trial lasted only about an hour, the length of the typical show. "Bob, you've been watching the tube too much. That's not reality. As I was about to say, the usual murder case takes well over a year to bring to trial."

"A year!" He was shouting now. "I can't stay in jail for a year!"

I said calmly, "C'mon Bob. Keep the faith. Hopefully we're going to find something that will blow a huge hole in the prosecution's case. Then we can revisit the issue of bail."

Sweat had appeared on his upper lip. "Sam. Please try. I don't know if I can make it that far."

And I believed him.

Chapter Five

I began visiting Bob at the jail at least once a week. Early on, at one of our prison meetings, I had requested that Bob give me a list of potential character witnesses who would supposedly testify to his upright reputation in the community. Originally there were twenty-three names on the list. I identified nineteen as belonging to our bocce team. I knew them to be as desperate a group as I've ever known. I mean, I love the Green Parrot and all, but not from eight in the morning until the bouncer, or "Dance Instructor" as they are called at the Parrot, escorts you off your bar stool, or floor, late at night.

During one of our bi-weekly phone calls—Bob was allowed to call me with that frequency at the State's expense—I asked him if any member of the team knew him better than others. I had not been aware of any particular long-term friendships. He admitted none did, and appeared disappointed when I told him I needed more reliable character witnesses. We finally culled the list to two names, after removing my name from the list for obvious reasons.

Since it was a Saturday, I decided to cold call them by dropping by unexpectedly. The cops use the same strategy when paying a visit to a potential perp—the earlier in the morning, the better. You want to hit 'em before they've had a chance to contrive a story. As far as I knew the two remaining names on the list had no idea they were included.

Peter Warren lived in the public housing project at Eaton Street and Palm Ave. Not a propitious beginning. I rang the buzzer at apartment 108 and waited. And waited. Then I realized I hadn't heard a buzzer, so I started to knock on the door. It opened before I could get my fist up.

There was no screen door, so my initial impressions of Peter were not mitigated by any shield, however slight. I smelled the stale cigarettes and booze before I could get to his eyes—which were bloodshot and framed in fleshy bags. I guessed he was late forties, and looked early sixties.

"Mr. Warren?" I queried.

"Yeah. Who's asking?" His voice reflected the years of sucking carcinogenic vapors through his vocal chords.

I explained who I was and why I was standing on his front porch. He didn't seem surprised and waved me in with a casual hand.

If his personal reek wasn't sufficient, the house made up for it. I almost gagged. But I persevered, got out my legal pad, and began asking him questions. He'd known Bob for all of two and a half years. They were basically fishing and drinking buddies. Peter owned a twenty-three foot Edgewater center console that he quickly told me was bought with the proceeds of a handicapped person lawsuit against his former employer. Seems the employer didn't take kindly to rampant alcoholism

Selfie

being a basis for showing up for work no more than two to three days a week. He thought Bob was a good ole boy and would be happy to tell the jury that. I cut my losses and moved toward the door after twenty minutes.

As I was leaving, he said, "Tell Mr. Selfie I said hi."

"Mister who?"

"Mr. Selfie. You know, Bob."

"Are you saying, selfie?" I spelled it out for him slowly.

"Yeah, you know, like when you take a picture of yourself."

"Well, why is he called Mr. Selfie?"

"'Cause he takes so many."

I had never heard this about Bob, nor had he ever mentioned it himself.

"That's interesting," I said, and I quickly took my leave.

The second listed witness, Sally Berkshire, was not home when I came calling. At least she lived in an upscale condominium development on Smathers beach. I followed a plumbing truck through the main gate, knocked on her door, and getting no response, left my business card with a handwritten note that I'd appreciate a phone call. I was just getting into my car in the parking lot when my cell rang.

"Mr. Harris?" a female said tentatively. It was a sultry, smoky voice. "This is Sally Berkshire. What can I do for you?"

"Ms. Berkshire. Please call me Sam. I represent Bob Wilson. He gave me your name as a character reference."

She made a sound that could have been a guffaw. "Oh, he did, did he? That's interesting."

I wanted to hang up, realizing this was probably a cul-de-sac that would lead me nowhere but a waste of my time, yet I persevered. "Are you home now? Could I come up to have a word with you?"

There was a brief hesitation, but she said okay and asked me to wait a few minutes while she put on something more appropriate. Momentarily I thought I had been time-warped back to a '30s Marlene Dietrich movie.

I hung the obligatory five minutes, plus two, outside of her unit, then knocked on the door. I jumped back when it opened before I had removed my knuckles from the surface. She was around forty, but a well-worn forty. Tall, around 5'10" I guessed. Self-dyed platinum hair was poofed dramatically atop her still pretty face. She was attractive, but in a saloon way. Being an accomplished drinker myself, I knew first-hand the cause of the blackish arcs under her eyes.

She led me into a larger room, past a small, well-applianced kitchen. If Sally didn't complete the Depression-era motif, the living room did. A pink Victorian-style couch sat just past a white wicker room divider. Overstuffed arm chairs, mauve and green damask, encircled the couch. Synthetic flower displays filled eye-level pots set in black, cast iron stands.

Ms. Berkshire was attired in what I would certainly call "something more appropriate." It was a shimmering white kimono embossed with vivid scarlet orchids, which generously exposed her breasts.

"Can I get you something to drink?" she asked.

She had already placed a small snifter of what looked like cognac by the table where she took a seat. I checked my watch. It was still morning. Well, it's five o'clock somewhere.

I declined and took the chair across from her because she motioned toward it. She sipped gently and asked, "How is the king doing?"

I paused, and then the reference came back to me. "As in selfie king?"

"Well, that too." Her cute mouth curved sweetly into a suggestive grin. "Did you know that Bobby has a size thirteen shoe?"

The non-sequitur initially stymied me, then I blushed in embarrassment. "Well, no, I didn't."

"He does, and that's why *I* call him king."

I continued. "As I'm sure you know, Ms. Berkshire . . ."

"You must call me Sally," she cut in.

"Okay, Sally. As you know, I represent Mr. Wilson on first degree murder, and other related charges."

"That's *so* wrong," she shouted and stood at the same time. Her kimono pulled upward, revealing more of her thighs than I wished to see. "I know Bobby. He'd never do anything like what they're accusing him of."

I wished I had consented to that drink now. Instead, I said, "I fully agree Ms. Berk...um... I mean Sally. I'm going to do my best to prove that."

"I hope so."

"As I mentioned, Bob gave me your name as a character witness. How long have you known him?"

"About three years. He picked me up at the Green Parrot."

I could tell the jury couldn't wait to hear more from Ms. Berkshire. "So, you became friends after that?"

She looked at me as if I had just disembarked from a spaceship from one of the moons circling Uranus. "You're kidding, right?"

"Ahh, he said you knew him well."

"We did *know* each other well, if you get my drift. But I have no idea where he came from, what he used to do, anything. We only discussed one subject."

I think I knew what that was. "What's your opinion of his credibility. I mean, has he ever lied to you?"

"Not that I know of. But I never double-checked anything he told me. We have what I would call a 'focused' relationship."

"Focused?"

"Yes. You know. Focused on one thing."

"Oh."

I stood up and thanked her for her time. As I was heading for the door, Sally asked what shoe size I wore. When I told her, she seemed disinterested, and turned away from me.

Selfie

This case certainly was not going to be won on the basis of our character witnesses.

Chapter Six

Over the next several weeks I researched the experts who would look over the evidence for us. The problem with having the government pay for them was that I'd be required to reveal their identity and any written results of their testing regardless of the outcome. If their final conclusions cut against us, we ended up providing additional experts for the prosecution.

Both the prosecution and defense lawyers have their own list of experts in any field. For the prosecution, it's usually those already on the State payroll, such as medical examiners, lab techs, and sometimes State Police who are specially trained in a particular subject matter. For the defense, it's doctors or professors from nearby hospitals or universities who have shown themselves to be sympathetic to those accused of crimes. The quality varies dramatically, as the bucks allocated by the courts are usually measly.

This was the first time I had handled a case involving DNA evidence. I called several attorneys in the area, and one gave me the name of Precision Labs out of Miami. I called, and was put on the phone with a Dr. Henry Gordon. I liked him right off the bat—friendly and a sonorous voice that exuded confidence and intelligence. I bet he'd slay 'em in court. I told him what I was up against and he suggested I get the State lab to send him the relevant DNA samples and results. We discussed his fee and he told me he'd email his standard fee agreement to me. I received it in my inbox six minutes after we hung up. His punctuality impressed me. It specified an hourly rate of two hundred and fifty dollars for his services with a thousand-dollar retainer. I signed, scanned, and emailed it back to him immediately. I also wrote a check from my business account and arranged to send it to him.

I went to see Bob in prison again on a warm drizzly day in August.

"Hey Sammy. How's it hanging?"

I had to admit, jail seemed to suit Bob. I mean, he looked great. He'd lost weight, not much, just enough to look fit and trim. His eyes were clear and steady. It was then I realized the relative unavailability of booze and drugs had cleaned Bob out.

"Very good, Bob. Hey, you look good."

"That's because I've got all day to work out, have to eat this crappy prison food, and am in bed at nine. Anything new on the case?"

"Not really. Still collecting evidence."

"Can I get out of here soon?"

"Don't ask that, Bob. You know the answer. You're in here until the jury acquits you."

"They're going to do that, aren't they Sammy? I mean I'll be found not guilty, right?"

Selfie

"I finished law, not fortune telling school. I'm going to do my best, that's all I can do. Have faith, Bob."

Bob seemed to be satisfied with that. We engaged in small talk for the next half hour—what was going on in Key West, the music scene, plentiful festivals—until I took my leave. Just before the guard arrived to take him back to his cell, he said, "Sammy, do you think you can get my cell phone back from the cops?"

"Your cell phone?"

"Yeah, the one they took from me when I was arrested."

I knew Bob owned a cell phone, but hadn't noticed that it was listed in the police inventory of Bob's property in the arrest report. I said, "You know you can't have one in jail."

"I know that. But it's got all my photos, addresses, everything. I could leave it with you or a friend and then have some way of getting the information I need."

"I'll look into that, Bob. In case I get it, why don't you give me your password?"

"Sure. It's 6969."

I should have known. Vintage Bob.

"And just in case I need it, your email address."

"The.selfie.king@gmail.com."

Chapter Seven

I hadn't been to my office in three days. Let me tell you about it. It's a conference room I use to meet clients. I get my name on a marquee, with many other names, and a gal who greets people when they come in. All calls to me go to my cell and I do most of my own typing on my home computer. If I get a big job, like an appellate brief, I've got a service that will do it. Low overhead, more money in my pocket.

I do get business mail there that I hadn't checked since the last time I was in. I also needed to pay my rent, which was quite affordable because I had represented the landlord's current wife, Donna Williams, in a rather unpleasant divorce three years ago. She was a slow payer so my landlord discounted our rental arrangement. Donna also happened to be the receptionist, toilet cleaner, and everything else he might want her to do. I never told him, and I trust she hadn't, that we had a wild affair during the first year I represented her. I always assumed that was why she didn't feel she had to make timely payments. A simple call to the Florida Bar would have put me in a sticky position.

She wasn't in when I arrived. I was a little disappointed as she was a real looker, had great wheels, and I always held out the hope she would again entice me into a hormonal-driven, coupling frenzy. My mail was usually left in a small bin to the far left of the counter. It was there so I grabbed the rubber-banded packet and left $200 in cash in an envelope with her name on it on her chair. I always try to deal in cash, and insist on it from my private clients. So far, the IRS hasn't found a way to place a lien on cash, but I'm sure they'll figure it out someday.

Back in the car, I leafed through the mail. There was a brown letter-size envelope that had my name, but no address, either mine or a return, and no postage. It must have been dropped off. I opened it and found a memory chip wrapped in a Post-it note with handwritten instructions that said, "See #s 8, 9, and 10."

At first I didn't recognize the handwriting. My interest was piqued now. I went home and plugged it into the side of my computer. There were ten photos on the card that I could access through Google Photos. They were of the crime scene, but from the vantage point of a third party taking pictures of the cops and Medical Examiner as they went about their duties of removing the body and evidence. The eighth, ninth and tenth photographs were a sequence showing Detective Albury placing the two pieces of wood in an evidence bag. The s*ame* evidence bag.

It clicked. I *did* know the author of the note and photographer. It was clearly Ralph DiPiero, a friend and freelance photographer for many of the publications here in Key West, including the *Citizen* and *Konk Life*. I immediately dialed him on my cell.

"I thought I'd hear from you."

"When did you take these?" I asked.

"Take these what?"

"C'mon Ralph, the photographs."

"I have no idea what you're talking about."

"Well, why'd you tell me you knew I'd contact you? Of course, I recognized your handwriting."

"Sam, we're friends, but for the record, I know nothing about any photographs, and I certainly didn't give any to you."

Now I understood. He thought someone was eavesdropping on him. "Okay, Ralph. I got it. Can we meet somewhere soon?"

"I'll contact you," and he hung up.

Chapter Eight

It was time to place another call to Dr. Gordon. At this rate, I would run through my expert witness money from the State well before trial. Only once or twice had I been left holding the bag after prep and trial work had exhausted the State's largesse bestowed upon me for professional expenditures. It can get real costly—and fast. But I had no other choice here.

I got him on the second try. He was more available than most I had dealt with in the past. I had already emailed him the photos.

"Hello, Attorney Harris. What can I do for you today?" His secretary must have forewarned him as to my identity.

"Doctor, please call me Sam. I hate to bother you again so soon. Did you get the photos I sent?"

He chuckled. "No bother, Sam. I know you read my fee agreement. I carefully modeled it after a lawyer's agreement. I charge in increments of six minutes, and we're already somewhat into that, with a minimum charge of twenty-five dollars for phone calls. So keep on calling."

Despite the humorous tone, his voice was strong and clear.

He continued. "But I'm not sure I understand their importance. What do they show?"

"The two sticks of wood in the shots. They're Exhibits 16 and

17, the ones you tested for me."

"Sam, are you kidding? You mean the probable murder weapon and the other stick? The way I see it, they were placed in the same evidence bag?"

"Sure looks like it."

"Well, that raises the serious issue of contamination."

"That's what I thought," I said. "Can you tell me about that?"

"I sure can."

His voice was tinged with excitement. I loved it when my experts got motivated to help the defense, usually because of some idiotic mistake made by the cops.

I asked, "Isn't that called transfer DNA, Doctor?"

"No. Transfer is the normal process of leaving DNA on an object. Primary transfer, for example, is when someone touches something and that person's DNA is transferred to it."

I asked, "So, in other words, if the defendant in our case touched one of the wooden braces, as we know he did, and his DNA was found on it, as it was, that would be primary transfer?"

"Exactly. You can also have secondary, and although far less frequent, tertiary transfer."

"Okay, Henry. Take me through this slowly," I pleaded.

His voice evinced infinite patience. "Let's say Mr. Wilson had shaken hands with someone. Then that person touched an object. Mr. Wilson's DNA could be transferred to the object that way. That's secondary transfer." He paused, I assumed for my benefit. "It's rare, but it even goes further than that. If the second person came into contact with a third, in some cases that third person could transfer the first one's DNA onto the object. That's tertiary transfer."

"Jesus. That sounds scary. Now DNA doesn't sound as reliable as I thought."

"It certainly can be, but these additional forms of transfer need to be ruled out."

"So what may have happened in our case?"

"The possibility is that one or both the pieces of wood were contaminated by the other. Contamination technically occurs after the evidence is collected. It's accidental in most cases. In other words, a contaminated sample is one in which the DNA was deposited during the collection, preservation, handling or analysis of the evidence."

It sounded like he was reading from a scientific journal, but I knew he wasn't. "How could you tell if that happened here?"

"We can't exactly. But it sure gives you some fodder for cross-examination, doesn't it?"

"Yes, it does. Also, take a close look at the victim's shorts and the DNA on the murder weapon. The lab results I received suggest some unknown donor DNA was found on both. Very unusual, in my book."

"I agree."

We spoke for a few minutes about the players involved in the case. He was amazed that any cop would combine pieces of evidence in close proximity to one another. He also said he'd send me some sterile plastic bags in case I came across any evidence I might want him to test for me.

He ended with this parting shot: "Sam, I don't know you that well and you don't know me. From the sound of your voice, I'm guessing I've got a few years on you. So just a word of advice. Watch your back on this one. Every case I've dealt with that involved this level of carelessness in the handling of evidence has also disclosed some level of shenanigans on the part of the police. Or worse."

"Thank you, doctor," I said. "Good advice."

****

I needed to get together with Ralph to talk about the photos. I knew he liked Sunset Pier, a restaurant on a wharf that jutted out into the Gulf of Mexico from the northwestern corner of the island. Tables with umbrellas extended the hundred-foot length, allowing privacy at the far end. We met for lunch. They served a great conch ceviche. Ralph had recently retired from his thirty-year local government job and was now exclusively pursuing his lifelong passion for photography. His freelance work for local publications was mostly just that—free.

We talked about his newest book on the local music scene—his second love was the rock, blues, and jazz that permeated our town. Ralph answered, when I asked him about how he found out about Frances' murder, "Yeah, I heard about the discovery of the girl's body on my police monitor. I ran right over. They had removed the body but were still working the scene. For the first time ever, I was initially kept away from the area by a cordon of uniformed cops. Very hush-hush. Finally, Officer Carney, a good friend of mine, allowed me under the crime tape. I could tell most of the others didn't want me there, especially Albury, who I photographed collecting some of the evidence."

I thought I'd dance around the issue and let Ralph raise it if he wanted. "Why do you think they were so cautious about who was there?" I asked. "I mean, they all know you."

Ralph looked around us. Not seeing anyone he knew, he said, "I'm sure it was because it was a fellow officer's child. But the carelessness I saw in the management of the scene did surprise me. Never seen anything like that." Ralph winked at me.

"You'd think they'd be extra-special cautious," I said.

"Yeah you would."

Chapter Nine

A day later I was on South Roosevelt Boulevard, heading toward the Triangle, as the locals call the main intersection going in and out of town, when I heard the siren. The speed limit on South Roosevelt is thirty, and I'd learned to set my cruise control to that speed because of the routine speed traps along the way. So I knew I hadn't been going too fast.

I pulled over immediately. It was a motorcycle cop. I didn't recognize him because of his dark-tinted visor. He didn't remove his helmet as he approached my window, which by now was open. I was suddenly aware of the blast of ninety-degree heat.

He lifted the face covering on his helmet. "Well, good day, Attorney Harris. How are we today?"

Oh shit. My stomach flipped. It was Officer Stearn. I knew him well. A bad apple of the force. One of several, as I was learning. He had recently been involved in an ongoing investigation into the death of an elderly man who had the presumptuousness to lead the police on a slow-speed chase. The incident ended with Stearn and two other officers holding the sixty-seven year old gentleman's face in the sand at South Beach until he suffocated.

I held out my license and registration, which he dismissed with a cursory wave of his black-gloved hand. "I asked you a question, Attorney Harris." His voice had by now assumed a command tone.

"I'm doing just fine, Officer Stearn. What can I do for you?"

For whatever reason, I said this in a high-pitched, sing-song tone.

"Get out of the car, Harris."

"Am I under arrest, Officer?" I was more serious now.

"You will be if you don't get out of the fuckin' car."

This was the second time in a month. I knew better than to take a stand now. I exited my car and he pointed me toward the wide sidewalk that runs along the ocean. He began to pat me down.

"Stearn, you must know I'm well-versed in civil rights litigation." Out of my peripheral vision I saw him toss a glassine bag containing a white substance on the concrete.

"My, my. What do we have here, Attorney Harris?"

I didn't like where this was going. At all.

"What, cat got your tongue, Harris?"

"Fuck you, Stearn."

He bent and picked up the packet. "I bet we've got heroin in here, Harris. How much you want to bet?"

"Fuck you twice, Stearn."

He looked quickly up and down the road, then with two knuckles extended from his fist, gave me a quick punch to the solar plexus. My body reflexively recoiled, and I had to gasp for breath. I tried, but couldn't speak.

"Just a reminder, Harris. If that dirt-bag Wilson gets off, your stay in Key West will be a living hell." He turned back to his bike, mounted, looked back, shot me a vicious grin, then lowered his visor. He blasted off at full throttle, only after giving me the middle finger salute.

Now I was shaken up. Stearn was enough of a loose cannon to truly scare me. I stood on the sidewalk trembling. My gut screamed for mercy. Slowly I made my way back to my car and headed to the Hogfish Grille on Stock Island where I planned to have lunch and drink the rest of my afternoon away.

Chapter Ten

I awoke the next morning with my head and stomach roiling. But I had work to do. After a quick OJ and cup of instant coffee, I went back to the police reports. I was particularly interested in the inventory of personal property taken from Bob at the time of his arrest. I hadn't more than glanced at it on the first go-around. Sure enough. There it was. Neatly placed in the middle: *"iPhone."*

I went to my computer and quickly typed a "Motion For Release of Evidence." I jumped on my bicycle and rode the six blocks to the Courthouse. It was time to pay Dan another visit. He hated it when I just showed up. Which is exactly why I always did it.

As I entered the reception area, I waved excitedly in Dan's direction, and said loudly, "So glad to see you, Dan." I knew he couldn't hear or see me. Cheri rose in a brief protest, but I continued my parade into the office area. As I approached I could just catch a glimpse of the pornography Dan was watching on his computer.

"Hey, Dan, how are you?" I said cordially as I entered his office.

He visibly jumped several inches out of his seat and immediately turned the computer screen away from me. "What the fu . . .?"

I cut him off. "Looking at photos of the family again?" I plopped down in a chair in front of his desk.

"How'd you get in here, Harris?" he demanded.

"Oh, I have special privileges in here, don't you know? Just like you think you have a privilege to withhold evidence from the defense. Time to have a little chat, Dan-my-boy."

"What are you talking about, asshole?"

"Bob Wilson's cell phone. You're holding it without giving access to the defense." I was trying hard to yank his chain now.

"It was on the inventory list. You can file a motion anytime you want to see it."

"I thought you'd make me go to court to get it back, so I typed one at home." I handed him my Motion. "I've marked it for hearing a week from today. Is that adequate notice, Dan?"

"See you in court, Harris."

The day before the hearing on the motion a hand-delivered package arrived at the office. Donna called me to let me know there was something for me. I headed right down, picked it up, and brought it back home. It contained an iPhone. I knew it was Bob's. It had just enough of a charge to turn it on. I punched in the password. The only apps visible on the home screen were the system apps—Settings," "Contacts," ones you couldn't delete. I searched for photos, text messages, anything that may have been there when they seized the phone. It was wiped. Nothing remained in the memory of the phone.

Selfie

Those fuckers, I thought. I knew it had to be shown to Bob, which could only be done outside of the prison. I had already made sure he was to be brought to court for the hearing on the motion, so I'd talk to him tomorrow.

I met Bob the next day in the courthouse lockup, with his phone hidden in my briefcase. Here the court officers were more lax.

"Hi Sammy," he asked me through the bars. "How's it hanging? How's Harley? Why am I in court today?"

I had sent him a copy of the motion and certificate of service to Dan marking the motion for today. I was sure he'd get it through the prison snail mail in the next month. "Hi Bob. Hangin' good. Harley's great."

I motioned for him to the front corner of the cell, away from the prying ears of the two other prisoners. "Several days ago I sent you the copy of the motion that was on for today. I knew you probably wouldn't get it in time. It was a motion to get your cell phone. But they delivered it to me yesterday."

I surreptitiously pulled it out of my bag, covering it with my hand as best I could. I brought it close to him and asked, "Is this yours?"

He started to grab it but I pulled it away from him. "Bob, I can't let you touch it . . . even for a second. Definitely against the rules." I turned it on.

"Looks like mine. What's it got on it?"

"Nothing, Bob. They wiped it clean."

He looked startled. "What do you mean? Where are all my photographs?"

"They're gone, Bob." I'd never seen him look so dejected.

"All of them? All of my selfies?" He was almost crying now.

"Yeah, as far as I can tell."

His shoulders visibly slumped. "I had hundreds in there. Going back for a long time."

"I'm sorry Bob. I'll make a stink about it to the judge. I'll even file a motion to dismiss the charges based on prosecutorial misconduct, but please don't get your hopes up on us winning that. There's nothing the court can do to get them back if they've all been erased."

We stood in silence for a half minute. I asked Bob, "When's the last time you took photos on the thing?"

"Right up to the time of my arrest. Sam, we've never discussed this. I don't know why. But I take a lot of selfies. Especially when I'm with Harley. I love that dog." Bob's voice audibly cracked. "They help me keep track of where I've been, who I've been with. I don't have the best memory. My photos are my memory."

"Well, again, I'm sorry." I did feel bad.

Just then one of the other inmates came over. I didn't see him until he was right next to Bob.

I said, "Hey buddy. This is a confidential attorney-client discussion."

"I know, I know," he said.

He was in his twenties, and did not look like the standard fare in the courthouse lock-up. He was clean-shaven and had an intelligent look in his eyes.

He continued, "I couldn't help but overhear the last part of your conversation. Something about a cell phone being cleared of its memory?"

"As I said, this is confidential."

"Yeah, but I've got a friend who may be able to help you. He's brought back some things on my phone that I thought I had lost. If the phone's an iPhone, he might be able to find it on iCloud."

Bob and I looked at each other. I had heard about the "cloud," but not the "iCloud." Bob looked equally stymied. "I'm sorry. What did you call it?"

"iCloud. It's the massive back-up system Apple uses to save your information from your iPhone . . . including photos."

"Well, how do you access iCloud?" I asked. I looked at both the young man and Bob as I said this, hoping Bob might come to the rescue. He still looked like he didn't have a clue.

"Tell you what," the guy said. "Give me your business card and I'll have my friend call you."

It couldn't hurt to give him my card. Who knows, it might lead to new business, so I gave him one. Bob and I chatted for a few minutes, and I returned home.

My phone rang an hour later. The caller asked, "Attorney Harris?"

"Yes. Who's this?"

"This is Cody Thurston. A friend of mine gave me your number. You met him in jail today."

"Oh, yeah. I remember."

"I understand you lost some information on your cell phone."

"Well, in reality, it was a client's phone."

"Was it an iPhone?"

"Yep."

"I think I may be able to help you retrieve whatever information you lost, if you want me to."

"How much is this going to cost me?"

"Tell you what. You meet me somewhere, let me see the phone, and I'll tell you honestly if I can do anything, and If I can, how much it will cost."

I liked the guy's voice and his demeanor over the phone. I imagined that he looked similar to his jail friend—youngish, good-looking, computer savvy. We agreed to meet at Harpoon Harry's on Caroline Street, the best breakfast joint in town. I told him I'd be wearing a straw hat with a colorful parrot band—my favorite, a Panama Jack.

He found me at the counter, and we retired to a table in the back. He was carrying what looked like a computer bag. Harry's is small, has every breakfast dish imaginable, and you can get a bloody mary or mimosa inside the restaurant, or a pint of rum at the connected package liquor store, any time of day. Real Key West. Impossibly, he looked just

Selfie

as I had pictured him. Maybe a bit taller and handsome, but in his twenties and on the nerdy side.

We ordered—he the corned beef hash and poached eggs, me the house omelet, a consortium of every vagrant tidbit in the kitchen. We talked sports for the first few minutes and into the meal—he was an aficionado of the local high school football team, appropriately called The Conchs—when I took out Bob's cell phone and placed it in front of his plate.

"Here it is," I began. "As far as I can tell, any information it had has been erased. I can't find a text message, photo, or anything. My client claims he had a ton of photos stored on it."

"Let me take a look." He picked it up and powered it.

I told him the password. He began tapping the screen furiously.

"Yep. Somebody went through this thing carefully and erased all the info. Did the cops know the password?"

"Not that I know of."

"Then it had to be done professionally. Do you know your client's email?"

I gave it to him. He spent another two minutes hitting various icons, his tongue stuck in one side of this mouth as he worked.

"Okay, I'm going to have to access iCloud from my computer. They erased that app as well."

He pulled a gleaming, paper-thin Mac from his bag and set it up on the table in front of us. "You get to iCloud on the net, and type in the email and Apple password to the account you're trying to access. Harry's has a free wi-fi network."

He turned the Mac so I could also see it and punched some more keys. "What's your client's email?"

I told him.

"Okay, let's try the same password." A screen appeared with Bob's name on it. The Calendar, Contacts, and Photos icons appeared. He clicked and Bob's Albums began scrolling down the screen.

"Looks like we've got them. They didn't go to the trouble to try to delete the photos from your client's iCloud account. It's difficult to do, but a professional could do it."

"Could you scroll to the more recent shots?" I asked. "There should be some of the Bridle Path over by Smathers."

He did, and I stopped him when I could make out the Bridle Path area in the background. Bob certainly was into selfies. It seemed every frame included Bob and Harley.

Cody looked surprised. "Isn't this the area where that little girl was raped and murdered a couple of months ago?"

"Yeah, it was. Could you email me all of the pictures which have the mangroves and salt ponds in the background?"

"Sure. You mean these Bridle Path photos?"

"Yeah. Those. I also insist on paying you for your services. How much do you want?"

"This was too easy. How 'bout you just pay for breakfast."

"That's more than fair."

Rusty Hodgdon

"I know I shouldn't ask, but what's this all about?"

"You're right Cody. You shouldn't ask."

Chapter Eleven

Over the next several days I needed to put out some fires that had been smoldering while I was devoting myself to Bob's case. One was a personal injury lawsuit that had been scheduled for trial six times, and which I'd successfully continued on each occasion. The clients, Steve and Roseanne Jones, were understandably upset. The next trial date was two days away and I had to meet with them to prepare for it. I called them and set up a conference for the next day.

I represented them in a slip-and-fall case. These were normally the weakest kinds of injury cases. Rosy, as she liked to be called, had slipped on a plantain peel outside of a very popular Cuban market here in town. Only the husband and one patron saw the incident. She fell hard but got up and continued home. When the pain in her butt only increased, she went to the ER and found out her coccyx was fractured.

This slip-and-fall was an especially difficult one. There were no photographs of the guilty peel and no one knew how long it had been there. The insurance company offered to settle for five hundred dollars, which my clients promptly rejected. It also didn't help that Rosy weighed well over three hundred pounds, her husband a good hundred more.

At our meeting, I went over their expected testimony carefully. We had also made a claim for loss of consortium on behalf of Steve, which in legal parlance means a loss of society and companionship, including sexual relations between the couple, caused by the injury. In my proposed questions, I focused on the fact the pair had not been able to take their normal walks and Sunday drives up the Keys for some time. I stayed away from the sex because the clients seemed to be uncomfortable with it. We left it that Rosy would say their sex life suffered.

If there is one truism about trials, it is that no matter what the degree of preparation, major surprises always occur. Rosy testified, then Steve. The direct examination went without incident.

Then defense counsel had his shot. I think he sensed blood. The following questions and answers occurred between him and Steve.

"Mr. Jones, you have made a claim for loss of consortium in this case, have you not?"

"Yes, I think that's what it's called."

"You know that includes a reduction in your sexual relations?"

"Yes, I do, and there certainly was after the accident." Bob's enormous frame filled the witness box.

Defense counsel approached closer to Steve. "Well, let's explore that, Mr. Jones."

I saw the jury look carefully at Mr. Jones, then again at Mrs. Jones. A noticeable tittering swept across the jury box.

"Ah, okay."

Selfie

"How often did you engage in sexual relations before the accident?"

"At least twice a day."

The tittering quickly evolved into outright hysteria. One woman had to grab a tissue as tears rolled down her face. Even the judge had to duck below his bench.

I was humiliated. Neither of my clients had ever before suggested such promiscuity to me.

"Mr. Jones, you're claiming, under oath, before this jury," and he swept his arm across the jury box, "that you and your wife had sex twice a day before the accident?"

"That's exactly what I'm saying."

Steve would not back off from this obvious exaggeration. I glanced at Rosy, who was clearly mortified by her husband's testimony.

Defense counsel was unrelenting. "How did that frequency decrease after the accident?"

"To once per day."

There was no holding back the squeals of laughter that engulfed the courtroom. The judge hammered his gavel harshly against the dais, called for a much-appreciated recess and scurried through the door behind him to his chambers.

During the recess, I convinced my clients to let me try to settle the case. The insurance company wouldn't budge from its initial offer, so I offered to waive my fee if they would accept it. I told them I was as certain as I could be in any legal case that they were going to lose this one. They reluctantly agreed and we settled, and I tried as best I could to push to the back of my mind the thirty to forty hours of legal work I had unexpectedly donated to the cause.

When I left the courtroom, I noticed there was a call from Sally Berkshire. I didn't listen to the voice message and just called her back.

"Hi, Sam."

I guess she had also entered my name into her contacts.

"Hey, Sally. You called?"

"Yes. I think I may have some information that you might find useful."

"What's that? Has something happened to Bob?"

"No. But it's about his case. I'm a little reluctant to discuss this over the phone. Would you mind coming over to my place?"

I didn't trust Sally and didn't want to be embarrassed by a come-on. I just wasn't interested. "How about my office?"

"No, Sam. I'm not dressed to go out. I'll make it worth your while."

I wasn't sure what she meant by that, so I hesitated. "Umm . . . all right, Sally. I'll be over in a half hour." I rode my bike over to her place. She buzzed me in the front gate, I locked my bike, and took the elevator to her unit.

She was wearing the same skimpy kimono. She looked better—less make-up and well-rested.

"Hi, Sam. Come on in," she cooed.

"I can only stay for a minute. I've got court in an hour." A damnable lie.

"Relax. This will take less time than that." She motioned for me to have a seat on the flower-printed love seat to the left. To my total dismay, she sat next to me. *Right* next to me.

I think because she sensed my discomfort, she smiled and said, "Don't worry, Sam. I'm not coming onto you. I just want to show you something."

She pulled out a cell phone and started scrolling through some photographs. "Here's some of me and Bobby. I like to use the narcisstick with him . . . he's so big."

I was shocked to see Bob lying in bed with Sally. Bob was completely naked, but Sally was attired in a French maid's outfit. I also had no idea what a narcisstick was so I repeated the word and asked, "What is that?"

"Oh, that's just my pet name for a selfie stick. You know, the poles that hold the camera at the end? In my opinion you gotta be narcissistic to always want to take selfies."

I looked at the photos quickly, not wanting to dwell on Bob in his full regalia. "Well, those are nice. But is that what you called me over for?"

"No. These are."

She scrolled to a different album. I looked intently now. It was of another naked man, not Bob. Sally was lying next to him in the same bed, dressed up in a very provocative little school girl's outfit—a short green plaid skirt, white blouse, open at the front, and white lace panties.

"Jesus Christ," I shouted. "That's Jerry Lathrop."

"Yes, it is. I didn't know who the father of your victim was until I saw the girl's name in the paper after you left. Obviously, Jerry is a good friend of mine."

"How good?"

"Real good. He's told me some things that I'd normally never repeat to anyone. But Bob's life is at stake here."

"Did he like you to dress like a young girl when you had sex?"

"All the time. I have several outfits, but that was the only one that would get him off."

" Jerry also brought a friend with him twice He was into the same kinky stuff."

"What'd he look like?"

Sally described a male, about Jerry's age, tall, good-looking. I immediately thought of Stearn.

"Man. And Jerry had a thirteen-year old daughter?"

"That's another thing I wanted to talk to you about. She's not Jerry's daughter. She's . . . I mean *was* . . . his stepdaughter."

"Are you sure? I've never heard that before."

"No one has, except his wife. They keep it a closely guarded secret. Even Frances didn't know. She thought he was her natural father."

"But she had his red hair?"

Selfie

"Sam. Trust me. Jerry dyes his hair. It's really brown, going on gray."

"Why does he do that?"

"Well, to cover the gray. But more than that ..." She hesitated.

"More than what? Tell me."

"Jerry's first name isn't Jerry. It's Michael. He assumed his brother's identification when his brother died fifteen years ago. You see, Jerry, or . . . but I'll call him Jerry for our purposes, was previously married."

"How do you know all this?"

"Men tell me things you wouldn't imagine. I bring it out of them. Mostly they're tortured by memories they've kept inside for years. They see me as a mother figure at times—maybe even a mother confessor. I know many of the intimate details of the lives of most of my male friends. In any event, he had two children by his former wife. When they were three and five and living in New York, allegations started surfacing that Jerry was sexually abusing them."

"What? Abusing?" I was yelling now.

"Yes. It got so bad a judge ruled he could only have supervised visitation with them. Well, the wife took the kids and moved to California somewhere. Jerry took on his brother's name and moved down here."

"Wouldn't the police have known this?"

"Apparently not. Jerry was the spitting image of his brother. The parents were dead, there were no other siblings, and Jerry easily slid into his brother's shoes."

"My God."

"My God is right. I'd have told you earlier if I had put two and two together—that the Jerry I know is Jerry *Lathrop*, the murdered girl's stepdad."

"I've been told he's out on disability. He's never looked physically disabled to me. Do you know what it is?"

"Oh, it's certainly not a physical problem. I've heard it's all mental. Exactly what, I don't know. But I've got to warn you, Jerry Lathrop is one sick bastard."

"Has he ever spoken to you about the murder?"

"Only sporadically. He said identifying the body was the most difficult thing he'd ever had to do."

"Why didn't the mom ID her?"

"You mean Betty Lathrop? Don't know for sure. I think she's afraid of him, so if he told her he'd go alone to see the body, she'd acquiesce. But I'll never forget the last thing he said to me."

"What was that?"

"He said that Frances looked beautiful naked . . . as she always did."

"He said that? She looked beautiful without any clothes on?"

"That's what he said."

Chapter Twelve

That night I had my first opportunity to check my email after meeting with Cody. The photos he sent were at the top of my inbox. His message said, "Call me."

I scanned through them quickly, noting again that Bob loved his selfies. Even though it was late, I called him. He picked right up. "Cody, this is Sam. You asked me to call you, but I also wanted to thank you for all you've done. I would like to pay you."

"I was glad to do it. But the guy you might want to pay is someone who could blow up some of those photos."

"Why would I want to do that?"

"Have you looked at them again?"

"Yeah, but only briefly. Why?"

"Do you have them available to you now?"

"I was just looking at them on my computer. I'm still sitting in front of it."

"Go to the third through the seventh photos in the sequence. Look at them closely."

"Ah, okay. What should I be looking for?"

"Just take a look."

I went back to the pictures and scrutinized the ones Cody had directed me to. I put on my 2.0 reading glasses, the ones Janine always said I looked silly wearing. Bob and Harley were in the foreground. But there was something else. As I progressed through the five shots, I saw a person. No, two people. In the far background. They were moving in the direction of the Salt Ponds. Was one of them carrying something? Sweet Baby Jesus. It looked like it.

"My God. I think I'm seeing what you saw, Cody. There're two figures in the background. Is that what you mean?"

"It is. But more than that. I think one of them is carrying a body. Looks to me like the photographer inadvertently captured the murder you're representing that guy on . . . or at least the dumping of the body."

"Are you kidding? I don't see that."

"I printed out the shots and put a magnifying glass to them. It looks like one of the men is carrying a young girl."

"Could you see what they looked like? I mean, any details?"

"A little. Hey, look. I've got this friend Tyler. An amateur photographer, but a genius at photo editing. Why don't I send him the photos and see if he can enhance them . . . you know, to get more detail."

"Cody, I appreciate all your help, but I don't want this floating around out there to too many people. Is there a chance I could meet with both of you to discuss this?"

"I'm sure I can set that up."

Cody called me back within an hour. "Tyler suggested we meet over at his place on Grinnell tomorrow morning. He's got his computer

Selfie

there. Why don't I download the photos onto a thumb drive and meet you there. Say around ten?"

"Sounds good."

He gave me the house number. I spent the rest of the evening printing out the photographs and studying them. I was so excited I downed five shots of coconut rum in a row.

I met them at Tyler's house the next morning. He lived in a small conch house on the northern end of Grinnell.

Tyler was large—not quite as tall as Bob, but stockier. He had red hair, but not even the remotest resemblance to Jerry Lathrop. Jerry had a crafty, sneaky look to his eyes. Tyler had clear, intelligent eyes that when focused on yours, were unwavering.

He introduced himself and led me into a small living room with a couch, chairs on either side, and an alcove to the left which sheltered an oaken desk with a large computer screen on it. Cody was in one of the chairs.

They explained that Tyler had already inserted the thumb drive into the computer but had not commenced any work on the photos. They were waiting for my arrival and consent.

We bantered about the weather for a few minutes. It had been unusually hot and humid for this time of year. Tyler pulled the remaining chair up to the computer next to a swivel office chair where he sat in front.

"Sam, I've got one of the best photo-edit programs out there. If we need high resolution versions of these photos, this baby will deliver them."

Tyler pulled up the first photo. He zoomed in successive stages well past the selfie of Bob and Harley, directly to the persons behind them. The two figures were a good twenty-five feet from the water. With each tap of the tab key, their faces gradually materialized in increasingly greater detail. At the last frame, I gasped. I knew it was Stearn and Lathrop carrying Frances' lifeless body toward the edge of the briny soup they called the Salt Ponds.

"Do you recognize these two?" Tyler asked.

"I think I know who they are. I'm not positive and I can't talk about this now, but how could I get good, clear, glossy eight by tens of these?"

"Do these relate to a case you're handling?"

"Yup, but again, I can't discuss it now. Can you get me hard copies of these?"

"I can have them ready for you in a couple of hours." He pointed to a large, expensive looking printer on a table in the corner. "How about five bucks a copy?"

"Great." I pulled twenty-five dollars out of my pocket and gave it to him.

"Stop by in three hours and I'll have them ready."

As I got up to go, I said, "Guys, I can't tell you why, but I really don't want you telling anyone about these photos. Is that a promise?"

"Well, sure," Tyler said. "But the tone of your voice is scaring me. Are we in any danger because of this?"

"You won't be as long as you don't mention it."

I left and headed home. I thought, in only two days, Jerry Lathrop had, as far as I was concerned, become a prime suspect in his stepdaughter's murder. And his buddy Stearn was an accomplice. Or at the very least, Bob who was standing clearly in the foreground of the pictures, could not possibly have had anything to do with the apparent crime in the far background.

Chapter Thirteen

Now I *had* to get a verified DNA sample from Jerry Lathrop. I needed a private investigator for the task. I'd been holding off hiring one because the court funds had been largely depleted with the other DNA tests and consultations. But I also rarely used one, normally preferring to pursue leads on my own. I got much closer to the guts of the case that way.

This situation mandated I back off personally. Jerry Lathrop was a cannon, primed, armed and ready to explode. He knew what I looked like. I required someone anonymous and with muscle. I knew just the man for the job.

His name was Emmanuel Gonzalez, a Cuban who had singlehandedly sailed a home-made craft from Cuba to Key West about fifteen years ago. We call them "chugs" down here, primarily because most have pre-sixties automobile engines for propulsion. Emmanuel's was different. His fourteen-foot catamaran was purely a sailing vessel, with the two hulls made of foam-stuffed, Navy surplus ammunition canisters, held together with baling wire and duct tape. A sail composed of sewn-together bed sheets provided the propulsion. It was a marvelous, if not foolhardy, race across the Florida Straits ahead of the

Selfie

Cuban gunboats that were looking for him. His boat still rests on the side lawn of the Botanical Gardens on Stock Island, together with many other such handcrafted yachts of myriad descriptions.

Before his emigration, Emmanuel had been a detective with the National Revolutionary Police Force, working out of Havana. Since his arrival and citizenship due to the wet foot, dry foot policy of the United States, he had become one of the premier gumshoess in the Keys. He was clever and fearless. He also had an arsenal of weapons, all properly licensed and obtained, which he brandished with astute timing without ever having to fire a shot.

I called him and he agreed to meet me at Sandy's Café, the Cuban coffee and sandwich place on White Street. As usual, he was attired entirely in black—trousers, long sleeve shirt, and a fedora. With his slick onyx hair and mustache, he was as sinister and frightening a figure as money could buy. As I said, he'd never had to fire a shot.

I arrived first and sat on the outside patio on one of the chrome and red vinyl stools.

"Hey Sambo," he said as he approached me.

I didn't like the moniker, but for obvious reasons never complained to him about it. "Yo, Manny," as he liked to be called. "Long time no see."

"Si, hace mucho que no nos vemos," he repeated back to me.

"How's Senora Charo?" I had only met his wife twice, but recognized she was undoubtedly the most beautiful woman on the Island.

"Always spending my money, so nothing's changed."

He ordered an espresso and Cuban cheese toast and took the stool next to me. "So, what's this all about?"

I had only given him the basics over the phone. "I need a DNA sample from someone."

"Why don't you just follow the hombre around and wait until he discards a cigarette, a cup, or something with his saliva on it?"

"Because he knows me, and I think I'd be in deep shit if he caught me following him."

"Who is it?"

"A cop out on disability."

Manny frowned.

I gave him Jerry Lathrop's name and home address, and a photograph I had found on the Police Department website. The name didn't register with him. I gave him one of the sterile plastic bags provided by the lab. "Put whatever you can get in this bag and seal it. If you can get a photo of him touching whatever you grab, that would be great."

"I'll do my best. But why do you fear this guy?"

I guess my attempts to disguise my disquietude about Jerry Lathrop had been unsuccessful. "The guy's nuts and has the backing of some of the other officers. I also suspect he has a terrible secret he doesn't want discovered. So be careful. *Very* careful."

Manny eyed me, shrugged, and made a circular motion with his finger around his temple. "Muy loco," he said.

Selfie

****

There were still other matters requiring my attention. I was representing a young mother who had lost custody of her child, Scotty. It was alleged she was harming the child. The Florida Childrens Protective Agency had placed the eighteen-month-old in foster care, determining my client suffered from Munchhausen By Proxy Syndrome. They had a psychiatrist who was ready to testify that Trudy Collins, my client, exhibited the classic signs of the disorder.

I had learned more than I cared to about Munchhausen. Mothers who suffered from it injured their children, often by suffocating them until they lost consciousness. They obtained some fundamental thrill, mostly the recognition and attention, of constantly having emergency responders and hospital personnel in their lives. Most women who lost their children to the disorder were never charged criminally with child abuse—the State knew most jurors had a very difficult time believing a mother would intentionally harm her own child. The FPCA claimed Trudy had strangled her child multiple times to the point of asphyxiation, then called 911 and become the hero when the child began breathing again. As in most of these types of cases, Trudy had medical experience. She had been a licensed practical nurse for several years, so it was reasonable to believe she could resurrect the child from an almost certain death.

But when this happened eleven times in ten months, and the doctors could find no logical physiological explanation for the episodes, she was examined psychiatrically and the diagnosis was made. So it was up to me to try to wrangle at least supervised visitation from the court. The problem was, Trudy adamantly refused to acknowledge she had a problem, and the judge had confided to me in his chambers that, for him, that was a prerequisite to allowing her to see her child. We were at an impasse.

Trial was looming—only a week away. On an early Tuesday morning, I received a call from Ed Warren, the attorney representing the FPCA.

"Sam, are you sitting down?"

I happened to be, with a cup of black Cuban coffee in front of me. "Yep. What's up?"

"Little Scotty was pronounced dead at 10:03 p.m. last night at the Lower Keys Medical Center."

I'm glad I wasn't standing. "What?"

"His two foster parents found him in his crib, blue, and not breathing. After they called 911, the foster dad tried to resuscitate him. It didn't work."

"My God. Is there any evidence of foul play?"

"No. the Medical Examiner has already ruled it a natural death. It was SIDS."

"Sudden Infant Death Syndrome?"

"Yes."

There was a long pause on the line as I collected my thoughts. I took a quick sip of coffee, which went down the wrong way and sent me into a hacking fit.

"Sam, are you okay?"

I gasped a quick, "Yes."

"It's the ME's opinion that this was the child's problem all along. He believes the prior history supports the theory, despite the professional opinions to the contrary."

"You mean it wasn't a Munchausen case after all?"

"That's what the ME says."

"Jesus Christ."

"Yep. Your gal is totally exonerated."

Yeah, but now, custody and visitation were very moot issues. "Thanks for the call, Ed."

I'm a chicken at heart. I called Ed back, but only got his voice mail. "Hey Ed, I was just thinking. Why don't you call Hillary Hutchins and have her go over to Trudy's house and break the news? She's better trained than I to do it." Hillary was the social worker assigned to the case. I could represent the most heinous criminal in the system, but could not look a mother in the eyes and tell her that her baby was dead.

Chapter Fourteen

A week after my meeting with Emanuel, an unidentified number showed up on my cell.

"Attorney Harris?"

It was a female voice, so soft I could barely make out the words. "Did you ask if this is Attorney Harris?"

"Yes, is this..." Her voice, still slight, was alluring.

"Sam Harris speaking. Who's this, please?"

"Charon Gonzales, Manny Gonzales' wife."

I immediately attached a face to the voice. A very good-looking face, at that. "Hi Senora Gonzales. How have you been?" I'd only spoken to her a few times in my life.

"Not well right now. In fact, I'm worried. Have you seen or heard from Manny recently?"

I had gleaned through the coconut telegraph, the vast gossip network that permeated the over three hundred bars in this town, that despite his wife's obvious assets, Manny was a player who regularly caroused the locales of Miami Beach. Often, I couldn't find him when I needed him. "I met with him about a week ago. Wait a second . . ." I pulled up the calendar on my phone. "It was last Friday."

"Was it for business?"

I interpreted this to mean it wasn't for personal reasons. I wondered why she asked. "I hired him to do a job for me. I can't say what."

"Oh. Okay."

I thought she might be weeping. "Charon." I decided it was all right to be more intimate. "I'm sure he's on an assignment. He'll be back soon."

"I know, but he's never not called me. Ever."

"Okay. I'll look into it. I know a lot of lawyers who've used him. Someone's got to know where he is."

"Thank you."

I was also somewhat concerned, even though I made sure to hide it from Charon. I immediately started making some calls. Left messages with five lawyers. Mentioned Manny and asked them to call me if they had any info on him.

The end of August brought in the steam. It rarely gets above ninety here—the ocean, which hovers right around eighty-nine all summer—palliates the otherwise onerous heat. The humidity is swimmable, and the lows plummet to eighty-six degrees at night.

Five days after the call from Charon a small article appeared on page five of the Citizen. The headline read, followed by the text:

HEADLESS TORSO FOUND ON MULE KEY

Two lobstermen found a corpse on Mule Key off the Northwest Channel yesterday. It reportedly had no head, even though the Medical Examiner determined it had been in the water less than twelve hours. The body was badly bruised. Identification is pending.

In the pit of my inner core I knew it was Manny. The sense of dread I felt at my first encounter with Jerry Lathrop was coming to a head.

Chapter Fifteen

The next day, Tim Hoffman, a lawyer I had known for years, called. "Hey Sam. Did you hear the news?"

"No. What?"

"You know that body they found over on Mule Key?"

Uh-oh.

"Sam?"

"Yeah, I know about it."

"They checked the fingerprints. It was Manny Gonzalez."

"Oh shit." My worst fears were realized.

Manny's funeral was at the Rodriguez Funeral Home over on Angela Street. It was well-attended by the Cuban community—not so much by the rest. I went and felt conspicuous. We gringo folk are rarely in situations where we're vastly outnumbered—in close quarters, to boot—by the Hispanic. It's a good taste of our own medicine.

It was a closed casket. I had a fleeting ghoulish thought of the funeral home director substituting a mannequin's head where Manny's should have been. I paid my condolences briefly, selfishly hating the way most people grieve their dead. Charon did not look me in the eyes. In fact, I felt a coldness that did not match my prior impressions of her.

As I left the Home, I was surprised to see two uniforms and what was clearly a plain clothes detective sitting in a squad car parked in front of the residence next door. Several flashes made it clear what they were doing—photographing people coming in and out of the Home. My first thought was, *why aren't you out looking for Jerry Lathrop?*

As it turned out, I had to walk by their vehicle to get to my bike. When I came close to them, the guy in street clothes stepped out. I recognized him as Officer Peters, one of the Florida State investigators in Bob's case.

"How are we today, Attorney Harris?"

"Just fine, Officer. What brings you here?"

"We always figure the perp of a killing will show up sooner or later for the funeral. Is that why you're here?"

I looked at him with incredulity. "What in the fuck are you talking about?"

He took a step closer to me. I could smell the stale odor of cigarettes on his breath. "Didn't you meet with Manny Gonzalez eight days ago?"

My mind was racing. I had counseled clients a thousand times never to talk to the cops without an attorney present. But hey, I was an attorney, right? Yet, as they say, a lawyer who represents himself has a fool for a client. I wasn't feeling too confident right now. "You know that's confidential information, covered by the attorney-client privilege, don't you Peters?" I was proud of myself for that quick retort, so my smile may have come off more like a smirk.

He took another step forward. I hadn't noticed it before, but up close he stood a good three inches taller than me. His spittle now danced lightly on my nose as he spoke. "Eat shit, Attorney Harris. We'll find out what you had to do with this, believe me. And when we do, it'll be my personal privilege to take you down. Hard." He turned and re-entered the car.

This had reached a crisis point. I wasn't going to take it anymore. I had no proof, other than my own personal experiences, that I was being harassed. But I had to fire a warning round.

The police chief was worthless. He'd back his own every time. I knew the prosecutor, Dan, would do nothing legally, but I thought he might tell the cops on the case to be very careful. The last thing any cop wanted was a federal civil rights action filed against him. Dan was a coward and wouldn't want to be in a position explaining afterward that I had cautioned him.

I went home and typed up a brief summary of my confrontation with Jerry Lathrop, Stearn, and now Officer Peters. I rode over to Dan's office, found out he was at lunch, and plopped down in the cramped waiting area. I told the receptionist I was there for the duration. I made a lot of noise turning magazine pages, talking loudly on my cell to several friends, and generally being a nuisance. I saw the receptionist go into a back office and make a phone call.

Dan strolled in minutes later at 3:15. His red, contorted face was as much anger as it was the libations of the day. His gait convinced me he was boxed. "What are you doing here?" he bellowed.

I stood up and gave him what I had typed. He didn't want to take it so I stuck it in the front pocket of his shirt.

"What's this?" he demanded.

I spoke loudly so most in the office could hear me. "Mr. Thompson, I'm giving you formal notice of my intention to file suit against you, the Key West Police Department, and the officers mentioned in this written summary. This document describes in detail the harassment I've received at the hands of the police. Send out the word to those named in it. If this harassment continues, it will only augment the damages I'll win through the suit. I'll next go to the Judge, the Mayor, and the Governor if necessary." I turned and marched out of the office. My paper was still sticking out of Dan's shirt pocket.

Chapter Sixteen

I pondered the issue for weeks. The last thing I wanted was to have a confrontation with Jerry Lathrop—or any of his other buddies in blue for that matter. I've never been a violent person. Have been in a few scrapes in my time, but I like to think they were unavoidable. At just shy of six feet and one hundred eighty pounds, I wasn't a huge man. But with four years of wrestling in high school, and three of jujitsu in college, I had learned how to handle myself. I had also managed, at least up to now, to keep myself in fairly good condition. But this was different. These guys had the guns.

By the end of the second week, I had arrived at a difficult decision. I couldn't ask anyone else to do my dirty work. This could be a crossroad in my existence—I needed to suck it up and do what was necessary for my client even though it might get me killed. I had to personally follow Lathrop to get his DNA.

I had never worn a disguise, as opposed to a costume. Key West was always replete with costumed revelers—so most people looked like they were wearing a disguise anyway. I thought blending in as a tourist would be the best bet. I bought a t-shirt at one of the five dollar shops that abound near the cruise ship docks. It said *I Got Duval Faced On Shit Street*. I also picked up some gaudy plaid shorts two sizes larger in the waist. I shaved the goatee and sideburns I'd had for over twenty years, dyed my hair black, and topped it with a baseball cap with "JOHN DEERE" stitched on the front. Lastly, I cleared my schedule for a week. With a small pillow tucked under my shirt at my mid-section, I had to agree most would not recognize me.

Armed with an instant camera, I rented a car and hunkered down in the early morning with several newspapers at the end of Jerry Lathrop's block on Twelfth Street. I already owned a set of small, high-powered binoculars. The car I had picked out had the maximum allowable window tinting in Florida, which made the interior nearly invisible.

At 7:45 I saw him leave his house and get into an older model Ford Crown Vic. I followed him at a safe distance to McCoy's Gym on Truman Avenue. The gym was the nastiest in town—open air, no AC—just overhead fans to blow the stench around. It reeked of sweat and cigar smoke. Yes, incredibly, there was always someone working out puffing on a fat stogie. It was often frequented by police and firefighters.

I stationed myself across the street in front of the gym. I pretended to take photographs of an historic building next to it. I visually followed Lathrop as he moved from the free weights to the machines. I hadn't noticed his musculature in the past, and was impressed when I saw him pressing a bar with two very large weights at each end. It must have been at least two hundred pounds. I kept a careful

Selfie

eye on a plastic water bottle and towel he carried around the large area.

I went into the adjacent store where I could still keep an eye on the gym. Forty-five minutes later he left, still clutching the bottle and towel. Shoot. It almost seemed like he knew he shouldn't leave anything that might contain his DNA.

I couldn't get back to my car in time to follow his trail, so I just headed in the same direction. Key West is two by four miles, so it usually doesn't take too long to run into someone again. I drove by the police station on Truman Avenue, but could not make out his Ford among the others.

I stopped by Sandy's Café for a coffee. The outdoor seating allowed me to survey the traffic. The problem was that Sandy's is primarily a locals' place, and I stood out among the Cuban men in their Guayabera shirts and the long-haired, unshaven residents.

I didn't see him coming. Jerry Lathrop strode up the steps no more than six feet from me. I turned away, and as I did I saw the Vic parked three spots down. I heard him order a Cuban sandwich. I didn't have a newspaper or other prop to concentrate on. Through the reflection in the car window in front of me, I could see him glance at me several times. A slow bead of sweat trickled its way down my back. *Did he recognize me? No way.* He returned to his car and drove off. Again, he left nothing usable. I thought this would be a good time to end my reconnaissance for the day.

I drove the rental eighteen miles north on the Overseas Highway to Sugarloaf Key. The Sugarloaf Lodge was just off the road. This is where Hunter S. Thompson lived when he visited. The room that he trashed was still labeled as such. Behind the hotel near the water was the Tiki Bar, a locals' place with a dubious heritage. I'd been there several times but it was doubtful anyone would recognize me. I didn't want to explain my disguise in Key West, where I'd surely be made.

I drank all afternoon, and after pouring myself into the car, drove home under circumstances that were both foolhardy and dangerous. I'm a good drunk driver—at least *I* think so—and set my cruise control to the speed limit. The problem was that I was only occasionally prepared for the numerous changes in the speed limit that occur on this stretch of the road.

The next morning, I retraced my itinerary of the day before, except I changed my hat to a Mets cap and my t-shirt to a white wife-beater. The shorts got toned down as well.

Jerry kept to the same schedule—straight to the gym at 7:45. This time I found a parking space directly across from the gym where I could see the inside through my shrouded window glass. Lathrop clearly was a man of routine. Same pattern around the room, same weights. Once again, he took his water bottle and towel with him.

I followed him in the car and pulled over past Sandy's when he stopped and walked up to the service window. I kept a close eye on anything he touched, but he left nothing behind. I kept up with him until he pulled into his street, then abandoned the day's efforts. This was getting much harder than I thought.

I was at my spot down from his house the next morning when I

Selfie

saw a gleaming black, new model Camaro pull behind me. Close behind me. Closer than it needed given the street space available. I watched it carefully. Through my rear-view mirror, I could see, but not clearly, two figures in the front. My heart began pounding like a sledge hammer in my chest, but I stayed with it. 7:45 rolled by with no Jerry out the door, and a half hour later I pulled away. The black car followed. The windows, darker tinted than mine, offered no insights into who was following me or why. I roamed the town, going down rarely used, tiny lanes that Key West is noted for. The Camaro followed at a steady twenty feet behind me.

I considered going to the police station, then realized how futile that would be. I headed back to the Sugarloaf Tiki Bar, figuring a public place would be the best to have any confrontation, if one were to occur. As I headed north from the Triangle, the car continued straight onto North Roosevelt.

I was unnerved. Who was in the car? Why did they follow me? I was sure I knew the answer.

I repeated my performance of the day before at the bar and returned home at sunset. The Camaro was parked directly in front of my house, facing my way. It had its lights on and as I approached, it blinked its brights several times. I continued past the car, not looking, and parked two blocks away in a residential parking spot.

I didn't dare go home immediately so I walked the streets for two hours. At ten o'clock I peered down my block and couldn't see the Camaro. As I walked up to my porch, I saw an envelope stuck in the screen door. I opened it. It contained a single white sheet of paper with a handwritten message. It said:

> *Nice try, butt-hole. Follow me again and you'll see what happens.*
>
> *Your friend*

Chapter Seventeen

I was defeated. I couldn't tail him again. I wasn't that much of a hero. So much for the crossroad.

It was my date night with Janine. As usual we met at the Grand. She looked dazzling: her typically short skirt, that tantalized by revealing her pink lace panties when she sat down, was light blue this time, and she was topped with a multi-colored, shimmering blouse that did justice to her "D" cups.

I never discussed business with her, unless you'd include monkey business in that category, but I was completely nonplussed by my present situation. We gave each other the conventional peck on each cheek and ordered drinks.

After our meals were consumed—for me a fabulous Coq au Vin and her a walnut and Gorgonzola salad—I decided to confide in her. She had already commented that she thought it looked like something was bothering me. I had no idea what her reaction would be.

"Honey, yes, I am under a lot of stress." I gave her the shorthand version of my suspicions about Lathrop's involvement in his stepdaughter's death and my efforts to procure his DNA, then ended with, "I can try to hire another private investigator, but everyone on the island knows about Manny's death and that he was working for me at the time. There are those who feel I may have had something to do with it."

Janine listened, never wavering in her focus on my eyes. "Do you have a photo of this guy?" she asked.

"I do," and I pulled out the police website shot of him.

"Okay, so you know where he hangs out?"

"Somewhat. He hits McCoy's Gym, and then Sandy's Cafe, every morning starting around eight."

"No, I mean at night, silly. I mean, does he have any nightlife?"

I was embarrassed to say that, even after three aborted attempts at following him, I had no idea what he did in the evening. "I don't know. Never got that far."

She studied the photo carefully. "Where'd you say he lived again?"

I reiterated the address, then noting the intensity in her eyes and set of her jaw, I added, "Wait a second, sweetie, you're not getting involved in this. No way."

"Let's go home and screw," she replied.

And we did. The next morning Janine left for work and as I was cleaning up around my place I noticed the sterile bag I had placed in my bathroom cabinet was missing. My first thought was that Jerry or his cohorts had gotten in and taken it. But why would they take an empty bag? I assumed I had misplaced it.

Selfie

I paid my weekly visit to Bob. I hadn't told him about my discoveries concerning Lathrop—I didn't want to elevate his hopes before I had ascertained Lathrop's true complicity. Bob still looked good, in fact better than ever. He told me, with his marquee boyish grin, that he had started, with the Sheriff's permission, a bocce ball team at the prison. He and ten other inmates spent a week building the court, and a local charity purchased the bocce balls. He seemed less concerned about the progress of his case but I still assured him I was doing everything in my power to win it.

Janine and I met the following Friday for our repast and after-hours dessert. She arrived carrying a small, soft-padded cooler.

"What's that? I asked.

"A surprise. Let's wait until after dinner."

I found her unusually evasive when we began discussing our respective weeks. Finally, after we had ordered our favorite cognac—Grand Marnier—I asked again, "Okay, what's in the cooler?"

She opened it, keeping it next to her chair, and pulled out a plastic bag, the ones they give you at the local supermarket. She slid it to me under the table. It was freezing cold.

"What the . . . ?"

"Just peek into it. Don't take it out."

I looked at her askance. "Am I going to get bitten by something?"

"Just look."

I held the bag in my lap and peered inside. There was my sterile bag, very frozen. "Is this a joke?"

"Look at it carefully."

It was dark so I had to bend down to see inside. There was a blob of hard, opaque white material in the middle of the bag. I looked up quizzically at Janine. She smirked back at me. Suddenly it hit me. "Is this what I think it is?" I whispered.

She nodded, her eyes sparkling with bemusement.

"How did you . . .?"

"Never underestimate me, Sam. Or do so at your own peril." The wan smile had disappeared, replaced by a seriousness I had never encountered in her.

"I now know that. But how will anyone know—especially the court—that this," and I pointed down at the bag, "that this is Jerry Lathrop's?"

She pulled out her cell, scrolled through some photographs, and handed it to me. The initial shot was of Janine, sitting in what looked like, with the cheap prints mounted on either side, a hotel or motel queen size bed. She wore only a flimsy negligee. In the second shot, Jerry Lathrop had taken up a position next to her. He was naked. Successive shots saw them in various poses of intercourse, the last one including fellatio.

"I excused myself after that final shot and went into the bathroom where I spit out the results into that bag. Within an hour, it was in my freezer."

"Jesus, honey. If this pans out like I hope it does, I'll need you as a witness."

"I know you will. And I'm ready. That dude is a total fuckhead. All he wanted at first was anal. When I refused, he slapped me hard across the face. Twice. He's lucky I didn't use Pierre on him."

I knew Pierre was her name for the straight razor she always kept in her purse. "I shouldn't have gotten you involved in this. I'm sorry. Please be careful."

"I will."

That's exactly what Manny had said, I remembered.

Chapter Eighteen

I rushed home and placed the bag in the freezer, hoping none of it had defrosted. The first thing the next morning, I called Dr. Gordon, and, as usual, he picked right up. I told him what I had, omitting any of the salacious details, and he told me he had a courier service that could pick up the specimen and get it to him ASAP. I didn't mention Jerry's name but asked that he compare this sample with any unknown donor DNA found on any of the evidence. I also told him I didn't want anything back in writing. Within an hour, a panel van with the words *Confidential Medical Transportation* embossed on the side pulled up in front of the house. A man came toward my front door with a slick looking cooler in his hand—I had seen them before—very high-tech, with thick soft-padded sides and a small battery operated fan built in. I gave him the sterile bag and he gave me a receipt.

When I checked my mail at my office later that day I found a large manila envelope waiting for me. It was from the State's Attorney's Office. It's not uncommon to receive a slew of reports of various kinds from the prosecution just before the deadline for the release of all discovery materials to the defense. Hey, they're like the defense bar. It's

Selfie

chicanery, delay and subterfuge at every turn. That's what filled this envelope.

Most of them were just remakes of older reports, updated with minor details only discovered, or remembered, recently. But several were brand new. One consisted of a single page, a chunk of which was largely redacted. It was penned by a Lieutenant Milbury whom I knew to be with the Monroe County Sheriff's Office, and read as follows:

On July 14, I was finally able to meet with Betty Lathrop at her home on Twelfth Street. She had been reluctant to meet with me prior to this date. Based on our brief conversations, I thought this might be due to her poor psychological state following the death of her child, and the fact her husband had asked her not to speak with us. When I heard Jerry Lathrop had visited some friends in Miami Beach, I went to their house and got her to speak with me. The place was meticulously kept up and clean, because as Betty told me, her husband is fastidious about his appearance and surroundings. When I asked her about the day of the incident, she told me her husband was furious with Frances for taking off on her bike before she had cleaned her room. He stormed out of the house despite my pleas that he wait until he cool down. He was gone over an hour. I was surprised to see he had changed his clothing while he was away. He told me he had fallen in the water while looking for her. The clothing was brand new because the price tags were still hanging from the shirt and trousers. When I asked him what he had done with the old clothes, he pointed his finger at me and ordered me to shut up. He was highly agitated.

What did Betty Lathrop tell the Lieutenant, and why was it blacked out? My curiosity was more than piqued. When I couldn't reach Dan on the phone, I ran over to his office. I was getting used to barging in on him. He was, as usual, in his office with the computer screen turned away from anyone who might be nearby.

"What do you want now, Harris?" he shouted.

I threw the one-page report on his desk. "What's this shit?" I asked.

"What are you talking about?"

"Why is most of this report redacted?"

"Oh, that. When Lieutenant Milbury told me its contents, I concluded it violated the marital privilege, so I had it blacked out."

"Wait a second, Dan. That privilege only relates to conversations between a wife and her husband. Is that all there was in there?"

"I guess so."

"You haven't heard the last of this, Dan."

"Suit yourself, Harris."

I grabbed the page out of his hand and banged his office door shut.

I returned home to finish reading the materials recently mailed to me. The second document, which I had also never seen before, was longer. It also had an attachment stapled to it. As I read, dread crept through me. It referenced Frances' Schwinn bike. The cops had closely scrutinized it and several fingerprints were lifted from the handlebars. Some belonged to Frances, but the others had been sent to the state lab for comparison. The attachment was a report from Carl Atkins, whom I knew to be the State Police fingerprint expert. After a lengthy analysis of the swirls and whorls of the prints at issue, my eyes bulged as I read this concluding line:

> *I compared the submitted prints to those of the defendant, Robert Wilson. They were an identical match.*

Holy mother of Jesus. Bob's fingerprints were on the girl's bicycle? How could that have happened? Unless he was guilty as sin?

I moved on to the third and final report, again one I had never seen. It was penned by Detective Albury. Here's what this one said:

> *I received a call from Sheriff Randall at the county jail. He told me he had an inmate, Steven Baxter, in his office, and he felt I should come right over to speak to him. I did, and met with them. Sheriff Randall informed me that Mr. Baxter was serving a two to five-year sentence for forgery and check kiting.*
>
> *Mr. Baxter was a young man, I estimated about twenty-five years old, and presented himself as trustworthy. He told me the following: about a month ago, he had served several weeks of his sentence in protective custody because of some threats made against him by a gang member. While he was there he was placed in a cell next to a person he soon learned was Bob Wilson. He claims they became friendly, and would have long talks into the night. On a Thursday evening, and he thought it was August 15, Mr. Wilson told him that he needed to get something off his chest, that he trusted Mr. Baxter. He then went on to say that he in fact raped Frances Lathrop, strangled her to death, and left her body by the Salt Ponds. He said he had never done anything like that before, felt horrible about it, and just wanted to tell someone.*

I was used to jailhouse snitches. They appeared in every ten or twenty cases when your client was incarcerated after charges were brought against them. I never believed a word they said. Unfortunately, sometimes juries did. The good news was that you could usually impeach their credibility with their normally lengthy criminal records. The bad news was that the prosecution rarely acknowledged there was any quid pro quo for their testimony. Any deals would reach fruition long after they were off the witness stand and usually occurred with a hush-hush motion to reduce sentence which was rubber-stamped by the court. It was rarely decisive evidence, but in this case, there were just too many loose ends pointing to Bob's guilt.

I had to talk to Bob about this guy Baxter – *pronto*, so I drove immediately over to the jail without calling beforehand. I had to wait an hour because Bob was eating lunch in his cell. I didn't want to disturb him because they wouldn't serve him again until supper.

As usual he straddled a chair backward. "Hey Sammy. Geez, I've seen you twice in a week. What's up?"

"Bob," I said, in as serious a tone as I could muster. "One of the most important agreements we had between us when we headed into this mess together was that you would always tell me the truth. Whether it be good, bad, or ugly. Do you remember that?"

He looked worried. "I remember it. And I have. I have, I swear."

I handed him the fingerprint report. He took it and read the first several lines. "What is this saying, Sam? That my fingerprints were found on the bike?"

"That's exactly what it says."

"Well, it must have happened when I helped that young girl get through the sand."

"What young girl?" I shouted.

Selfie

"I must have told you. One day when I was walking Harley, a girl got stuck in the sand on the Bridle Path and fell over. I picked the bike up and got her on her way."

"You never told me anything of the kind. You don't think I would remember that?"

I had never seen Bob look so sheepish.

"I'm so sorry. I haven't thought about it since that day. I never realized it was the girl who was killed."

He looked and spoke so earnestly that I had to believe him. "Well, it was, and I don't know how we're going to explain that to the jury."

"I'll just get up on the stand and tell the jury what happened. They'll believe me, won't they Sam?"

"We'll talk about you testifying later, but I certainly hope they believe you."

"I . . . think they will," he said.

"It gets worse, Bob." Do you know a guy by the name of Steven Baxter?"

A glint of recognition shined in Bob's eyes. "Sounds familiar. Who is he?"

"He's an inmate here at the jail who claims you confessed the crime to him."

"What! What are you talking about?"

I handed Bob the one page police report, and watched his face contort in disbelief as he read.

"Sammy, I swear this never happened. I do remember a new guy about this age moved in next to me for a couple of weeks. but I never told him I hurt that girl. Never!"

I looked at Bob carefully. As I've said, you never know for sure when someone's lying through their teeth.

"Okay. I'll pull the jail records to see if he's telling the truth about being placed next to you. And I'll get his criminal record. But I can't begin to tell you how much all this hurts us. It hurts a lot."

"What are you saying? That I'm going to be found guilty?

"I just want you to tell me the truth. That's important to me. Did you have anything to do with Frances Lathrop's death?"

This was the first time I had directly asked the question of Bob. The most common question people ask me is, "How can you represent a guilty person?" It's a naïve question. First, I am not the judge or the jury—It's up to them to decide guilt or innocence. I also rarely ask a client if they committed the crime. If they say yes, I am then precluded from calling them to the stand to testify, even if I wanted to. Under the prevailing ethical rules, I cannot elicit testimony from a witness that I know to be false.

Also, I never really know if a client is guilty or not—the legal annals are replete with false confessions from defendants who, because of mental illness, pressure from the cops, or some other reason, admit to a crime they did not commit. Plus, I don't care if my client is guilty or innocent. My job—my only job—is to provide the best defense I possibly can. Then it's time to let the chips fall where they may.

Bob looked as if I had spit in his face. He reddened to a scorched maroon in a matter of seconds. A wild, atavistic fire formed in his eyes. Bob stood, hovering over me, and in a very loud voice said, "Okay. What do you want me to say? That I raped and killed that girl?"

"No, I don't want you to say anything but the truth."

"I guess you don't like the truth. So how about this? I fucked that poor little girl and bludgeoned her to death. There you go. Now do you have what you want?"

I wasn't able to stop him in time before those words came out, so I immediately stood and clapped my hand around his mouth, and said, "Christ, Bob, keep your fricking voice down. For God's sake."

He sat down, still shaking uncontrollably.

"I know you didn't kill her," I said. "Settle down. I just needed to tell you we've got a tough case now because of all this."

He didn't speak for almost a minute. The silence was unnerving, but I decided to let him speak first.

Finally, he said, "All right. I'm ready for anything. Let's get it on."

Chapter Nineteen

The next Friday Janine and I met again for our weekly date. Knowing how resourceful she could be, I brought the redacted report with me. Once again, she looked stunning. She had done something special with her hair—it was curled nicely around her cute face and was blonder than usual.

"You look great tonight, honey," I said.

She acted more demure than usual, and unlike her norm, accepted the compliment easily. What was up?

Our banter was especially pleasant. After we ordered dessert, she reached across the table and took my hand, again a first. "Sam, I've lost my lease on my place. The landlady claims she doesn't like my activities there. I don't care and I'm tired of the nosiness of her and her family. Especially the twelve-year-old son who keeps showing up at odd times."

Janine occupied the upstairs of a large home on Eaton Street. Even though she had a separate entrance, she had mentioned to me several times the intrusions of the owner and her teenage son, the latter showing an abnormal prepubescent interest in their only tenant.

"I think it's for the best too," I said. "Where are you going?"

Selfie

The glint in her eye provided the answer. "Sweetie, we've been together for a long time."

I gave her hand a quick squeeze, but withdrew. "Yeah, all of a year and a half." I didn't mean to say it sarcastically, and I saw her study my eyes to make sure it wasn't.

"I think it's time to move in together."

Now it was my turn to closely scrutinize her face. "Seriously, honey? You don't think we need more space than that? I mean, we've both lived alone for so long."

Her pouty mouth showed some disappointment. "I know, but I'm beginning to fall in love with you. Don't you think we could give it a try?"

Though I tried to smile, I wasn't at all sure I wanted to give it a try. I relished my privacy, and my quirky but ordered environment. But now that she was being so forthright, I was pleased to hear her express her feelings for me. It brought to the surface some of the deep emotions I had for her. All I could say now was, "Can I think about it? I mean, this is very sudden."

Her shoulders slumped. "Of course, take all the time you want."

I didn't like the timing for showing her the redacted report, but I was anxious to get her take on it. "Maybe this isn't the best moment to ask you this, but I do respect your opinion. And I know you have a way of figuring things out. I got this report—just recently—from the cops. They blacked out a huge chunk of it."

She sighed. "Okay, let me look."

Rusty Hodgdon

I handed her the report. She appeared relieved for the abrupt change in topics. "I've seen this done before." She placed her cell on the table and turned on the flashlight app. Hers was remarkably bright. She then placed the redacted portion of the report, face down, on top of the light. "It comes out backward. But this is the only way to reveal the words."

She reached into her purse and pulled out a pen and a small spiral notebook. Opening the notebook to a blank page, she handed them to me and told me to write down the words as she read. It was halting and slow, but I got it all down. The full report now read:

On July 14, I was finally able to meet with Betty Lathrop at her home on Twelfth Street. She had been reluctant to meet with me prior to this date. Based on our brief conversations, I thought this might be due to her poor psychological state following the death of her child, and the fact her husband had asked her not to speak with us. When I heard Jerry Lathrop had visited some friends in Miami Beach, I went to their house and got her to speak with me. The place was meticulously kept up and clean, because as Betty told me, her husband is fastidious about his appearance and surroundings. When I asked her about the day of the incident, she told me she had visited with her sister on Southard Street most of the day. When she returned, her husband was furious with Frances for taking off on her bike before she had cleaned her room. He stormed out of the house despite Betty's pleas that he wait until he cooled down. He was gone over an hour. When he returned, she was surprised to see he had changed his clothing *while he was away. Her husband told her he had fallen into the water while looking for Frances. She thought the clothing was brand new because she had never seen it before and a price tag was still hanging from the shirt. When she asked him what he had done with the old clothes, he pointed his finger at her and ordered her to shut up. He appeared highly agitated.*

When she had finished, it took me several seconds to tie my handwritten portion to the rest of the report and understand its significance. "Jesus, Janine. Are you sure you read that accurately?"

"I'm sure, and I think I understand what it all means. The stepdad was pissed off at his daughter, went looking for her, and she ends up dead. He comes home with different clothes on. Sounds like a murder suspect to me."

"Yes, it does. It surely does."

Chapter Twenty

I received a call from Dr. Gordon four days after having shipped the specimen to him. He initiated the conversation, "We have the results from the semen sample you sent us. By the way, where did it come from?"

"I'd rather not say right now. I don't want the prosecution to be able to subpoena you and force you to testify in their case-in-chief. I don't want any of this disclosed until we present our case."

"That's fine. The reason I ask is the sample contains the DNA from two persons—one an unidentified female, the other is from the same unknown donor on the shorts of the victim."

I muffled my excitement. "That's very interesting. I didn't really expect that."

He chuckled. "Somehow, I don't believe that, Sam."

"You've been in this business too long, Henry."

"What about the unidentified DNA on the stick of wood? Was it the same as the DNA I sent you?"

"Strangely, no. Totally different. You don't want a written report on this, is that how I understand it?"

"That's right. Let's just keep this between us."

"You got it," he said.

I was glad to hear Lathrop's DNA was on his stepdaughter, but that could have landed there through normal parent-child interaction. And what about the other DNA, which somehow introduced another man, or murderer, into the equation? I was convinced Lathrop was mixed up in the death of his stepdaughter and that he knew who else was involved, but the prospect landed me clearly on the proverbial sharp horns of a dilemma. Should I approach Dan with the results of this new testing and the photographs in the hope he might dismiss the case against Bob? Or try to hold it close to my vest to surprise him with it at trial?

If it was any other prosecutor, I'd lay it out in detail and possibly get a dismissal and a new indictment against Lathrop . . . or another. But Dan was different. His political instincts would not allow him to charge a police officer with this type of crime. If the cop got off, Dan's career would be over. And my case depended on some grainy, background shots at the Salt Ponds, and Janine's testimony coupled with the photographic evidence of a rather distasteful, at least to a jury, procurement of the sample.

I could file a motion to get the court to order Lathrop to give me a DNA sample, but that would also entail a full revelation of my case and there was no guarantee of success. I might have to reveal everything beforehand anyway. Reciprocal discovery required me to give the prosecution notice of what exhibits I intended to introduce and which witnesses I was going to call. But I had learned over the years to be rather clever in burying crucial information in a way that a not-too-astute prosecutor, like Dan, would understand its significance.

If I took this latter approach, it was not without some peril—I had seen it happen to others, and I almost fell prey to it once—the court's refusal to allow in critical evidence because it had not been made known to the prosecution in a timely fashion. I couldn't let that occur here.

I also feared for my witnesses' safety once their names were disclosed—especially Janine. Jerry must know her name, maybe even her address. I would not put her into any potential jeopardy, at any cost.

I decided it was time to meet with Benjamin Schultz, a local lawyer with whom I had become quite friendly. He was eighty-six and from the old guard, where lawyers behaved like gentlemen toward each other—not like the new clan, where everyone tried to rip out their opponent's jugular at every turn. It was a scorched-earth policy that had turned lawyering into a prolonged blood bath where no one ultimately won. I had turned to Ben before for advice when things got hairy.

Ben was one of the few Jewish attorneys in town. He claimed to be retired, even though he put in more hours at the office than I did. His wisdom and experience surpassed the collective knowledge of most of the attorneys in this county. Over his fifty-five-year career, he had taught occasional law courses at some of the most prestigious schools around the country.

Selfie

He agreed to meet with me for drinks at Louie's Backyard, a popular locals hang-out, which offered a top-notch restaurant with a deck bar that extended out into the Atlantic. It afforded some privacy and great views of the ocean.

He arrived in his usual attire—a rumpled suit with the jacket draped over his arm. It looked far too heavy for the season and the still low-eighties temperatures. His tie, a remnant from his college days at Harvard and food-stained in noticeable areas, was pulled down half-way to the middle of his partially unbuttoned shirt. It was only when he got closer that I saw two buttons were missing. His black, wing-tipped shoes, scuffed and scraped, completed the image of a college professor gone to seed.

"Sam, always a pleasure," he said as we took our seats at a high-top table.

"The pleasure's mine. It's been a while. How have you been doing?"

"Great."

Ben was always great.

"Just completed an estate plan for Charles," he said. "A real beauty. And a twenty-thousand-dollar fee."

I was already feeling ill. Charles Knowles was one of the wealthiest scions in Key West. Being a real estate broker and developer, he was primarily responsible for converting this town from a back-water collection of deteriorating wooden structures to its present assembly of stately historic homes and attractive condominiums and townhouse developments. Why couldn't I land those clients?

"Nice. All I get is the non-paying scumbags."

The sun was close to the horizon. Key West is noted for its spectacular sunsets. The aqua and cerulean waters reflect upon the sky and sunbeams to create an amorphous hue of indigoes and greens. Many people have claimed they have seen the so-called "green flash" at the very moment the sun sinks below the sea line. I know it's real—I've witnessed it twice.

"Is your present client—the one involved in that Lathrop matter—one of those?" he asked.

"No, not really. He's a friend."

"Oh-oh."

"No, it's okay. I was appointed to represent him. And I'd like to talk about his case with you, if that's okay." I handed him a one dollar bill, a tactic we all use to insure the confidentiality of our conversation. Ben was now a paid consultant. He understood exactly what I was doing, and took it with a wink.

"Anytime," he said. "You know that. But right now, I'd like a scotch and soda."

No modern drinks for Ben. We ordered, made small talk, and I explained exactly what I knew about Jerry Lathrop's possible involvement. I ended with, "So, as you can see, I don't want the prosecution to know I've got Jerry Lathrop in my cross-hairs. Not only don't I know what he'd do if he found out, but it would give the State time to prepare a parry to my thrust."

"You think Lathrop is a threat?" Ben asked.

"Yeah, I do. Both him and his cohorts."

"Okay, let's work on those exhibit and witness lists together. Carefully."

"Thanks for your help, Ben."

"Sounds like you need it, kid."

Chapter Twenty-One

As I thought about it, having Janine move in with me made a lot of sense. I had found myself suffering from some depression lately—didn't know exactly why, but I guessed it was because after fifteen years I was getting burned out in my profession. The law is a jealous mistress, and does not leave much space for other activities, especially relationships. Janine was the least demanding woman I knew, and I felt the arrangement might work. And, as she was becoming an increasingly important witness in the case, I could keep her close, and hopefully safe.

After a day, I called her and invited her to move in, with one major condition—neither of us could have a person of the opposite sex stay overnight in the house. She agreed, and arrived the next day with five suitcases, three boxes of knickknacks, and her cat Jerry Garcia. My guestroom was quickly turned into a Woodstock emporium, with posters of Jimi Hendrix and Jim Morrison adorning the walls, and a large, ornate hookah on a table by her bedside.

Over the next several weeks she turned out to be an ideal roomie. She kept to herself and isolated her messiness to her own room. We

Selfie

stuck with our Friday date nights, now being able to wake up on Saturday mornings together in the same bed. She occasionally disappeared for a few days at a time, always returning with something good for us to eat. I never questioned where she had been. Garcia and the two dogs reached an easy truce, but only after he had swiped Harley's nose with a sharp left hook.

We were in my living room one night when I asked her if she had ever gone by any other names. She appeared surprised by the question, but when I explained the reason why I was inquiring, she understood.

"We've never discussed this, but I was married for about a year out in California. A real mistake."

"Did you ever use his last name?"

"Yes, for the time we were married. I then asked the court to allow me to resume my maiden name, Williams."

"What was his name?"

"Reynolds."

"I'm going to put you on my witness list as Janine Reynolds, okay? I'm also going to draw up a short lease for you in that name—just so our arrangement looks more formal."

"Fine with me."

****

I met again with Sally to go over her probable testimony. I also wanted to ask her something. After we were comfortably ensconced in her living room, sipping cognac, I said, "Sally, I don't want you to take this the wrong way, but it's for Bob's benefit. I can't tell you why I'm asking it because the prosecution might get that out of you on the stand."

"You can ask me anything. I know you're the only thing between Bob and life in prison."

"All right. Have you ever gone by a different name? Maybe a maiden, or stage name?"

"Umm. That is a strange question."

"I know it is."

"Where do you want me to start?" she said with a sly grin.

"I guess where you want to start."

She took a longer than normal swig out of her glass. "I was never married, but have gone by a number of stage names."

I was surprised. "You've never married?"

A barely perceptible sadness clouded her eyes. "No, it wasn't allowed back then."

I looked at her carefully, not understanding. Then it came to me as an instant illumination. Sally was a guy. "I'm ... I'm sorry," I managed to stutter. "I just didn't realize ... ah, you look ... so ... good."

She looked at me with soft, moist eyes, appearing to empathize with my discomfiture. "So, I've danced and performed all of my life, mostly drag shows at the gay and trans clubs here in Key West – you know, Aqua, Bourbon Street, The 801."

"I understand." Man, it seemed that at every turn I was learning more interesting things about Lathrop – and Bob.

"Some of my stage names have been Lady Divine, Sister Boom-Boom ... and for a while, Hedda Lettuce."

"Okay."

"I was born Salvatore Graziano. When I was twenty I got a sympathetic judge here in Key West to allow me to legally change my name to Sally Berkshire."

"Do you ever still use Salvatore Graziano?"

She thought for a minute. "I've always kept a post office box in that name. Made it a lot easier for some of my family and their friends to communicate with me.

"Do you get any mail here in that name?"

"Yep."

"Would you mind if I listed you as our witness under that name?"

"I have no problem with that whatsoever."

"Would you remember to answer by that name if anyone calls you? Like the cops, or prosecutor's office?"

"Sure. Will they call me? And what should I say?"

"They might call you. And I can't tell you not to talk with them. But you have no legal obligation to do so. I usually tell my witnesses to simply say they have no comment at this time, if that is in fact the case."

"Okay, that's what we'll do."

"Also, and I'll be repeating this again once we get down to final trial preparation. If you're asked on the stand if we spoke to each other before trial, answer truthfully, and if he asks what I said to you, you simply say that I told you to tell the truth. Okay?"

"Got it."

"Also, Sally, be careful out there. *Real* careful."

"Got it."

Chapter Twenty-Two

It had been agreed between Ben and myself that I would prepare a first draft of the lists and meet with him afterward. My initial witness list included the original twenty-three people (sans myself) Bob had given me, all the prosecution witnesses, including cops, medical personnel, Medical Examiner, and finally, Dan Thompson.

As I've said, there's a lot of chicanery involved in these lists. I wanted to include as many people as possible in the hope the prosecution would feel compelled to contact all of them, thereby expending futile energy and time on the endeavor. The cops and Dan were added simply to make them wonder what the hell I was up to. Sally, as Salvatore Graziano, and Janine, as Janine Reynolds were there. Let 'em figure it out. Jerry and Betty Lathrop concluded the list.

Duplicating Bob's first list was not without its dangers. I was taking the chance one of them might say something stupid, or false, that the prosecution might use against us. But I doubted any of them would do that, and was relatively certain none of them would talk to the cops because of their learned distrust of them.

The exhibits were more complex. As with the witness list, I

would include all the State's exhibits, again to keep Dan puzzled. But how would I label the semen specimen from Jerry Lathrop? And the selfie photos? This is where I needed Ben's help. I called him and we again agreed to meet at Louie's. I brought an extra copy of my lists.

We went through the witnesses first. Ben questioned my inclusion of so many of Bob's acquaintances, but agreed with my overall strategy. He also approved of my legerdemain regarding the alternate names for the ladies.

We next turned to the exhibits.

"Looks like you've copied all of the State's exhibits, right?" Ben asked.

"Yes. My big problem is the body fluids from Jerry and the shots that we think show Jerry carrying his daughter by the Salt Ponds. Obviously, I want to give away as little as possible before we introduce that evidence."

"The prosecution listed DNA from 'unknown donors' in their exhibits, correct?"

"Yeah, one of which we now know is Lathrop's."

"So why not list the semen the same way?"

"Why didn't I think of that?"

"And they included photos of the crime scene in there, no?"

"Yep."

"List yours the same way."

"Brilliant."

"Have any idea who the other DNA is from?" Ben asked.

"I have my suspicions."

"Stearn? Well, whose ever it may be, it certainly diverts attention away from your guy, doesn't it?"

"It surely does."

Chapter Twenty-Three

I guess I should tell you how I became a lawyer. It certainly wasn't because of any early ardent desire on my part. My dad was one. A good one. Worked at a silk-stocking law firm in downtown Chicago. I always wondered where that term came from—silk stocking, that is. Sounds like a more apt description for the transvestite shows down here in Key West.

Growing up, I rarely saw him. He worked ungodly hours. But I never went without. A brand-new Corvette upon graduation from a top prep school in Evanston, full fare to an ivy league college. A small trust fund to make my way through law school. That was gone after my down payment on my place here in Key West.

The pressure started by my junior year in college. I wanted to major in female anatomy, but the threat of my dad yanking my college education funds found me quickly switching to poly sci. When he offered to pay full freight to Northwestern Law School, I had no choice. I was going to become a lawyer. I had the foresight to take both the Illinois and Florida bar exams. I had an early inkling that the mid-western conservatism and winters would not keep me there long.

Selfie

In the September following Bob's arrest, my mom called and said they'd like to pay me another visit. Quite a surprise considering they'd only come down once in ten years, that occasion being an unmitigated disaster. I couldn't say no—they'd never stay with me so it wouldn't be any inconvenience. My parents would rather camp out in one of the local parks than brave my cubicle of a home.

The first visit, I made the mistake of taking them to the Bourbon Street Bar for a drag show, notably one of the scummiest in town. When an extraordinarily well-hung stripper straddled the chair in which my mother was sitting, his dong hanging precariously inches from her face, they exited the establishment immediately and truncated their visit the next day, citing stomach problems as the excuse.

This time they arrived on a Wednesday in mid-September. I picked them up at the airport and took them to the nearby Hyatt with an agreement we'd meet for dinner. They had been to the Grand their last visit—long before I had met Janine. I tried to dissuade and steer them toward another eatery for fear we might run into Janine, but they were adamant.

The dinner conversation, because of a dearth of other topics, quickly turned to my cases. This was only after my father had rejected the first two perfectly fine bottles of wine, a practice that had embarrassed me immensely since early childhood. I started telling them about Bob's case. My mother was horrified that I would take a case involving the rape and murder of a young girl. My explanation that I was appointed to the case under circumstances where I could hardly refuse did not mollify her. My father, being a lawyer who had on many occasions made the necessary concessions in his moral integrity, was more receptive.

When I began to set out the major hurdles I faced in directing the focus of the spotlight upon the girl's father, dad became particularly interested. He had done some criminal work in his early days, and I think the blood and guts of this one brought out the old hunger in him. I spoke in layman's terms for my mother's benefit.

"So, I've got to get into evidence Jerry Lathrop's conversation with his wife about his whereabouts on the day of the killing. It's critical. Then I run into both the marital testimonial privilege and the marital communications privilege."

I caught my father quickly glance at my mother's quizzical expression, and he cut in: "Beth," he said solemnly, "what he's saying is the law generally recognizes that private conversations between spouses should not be admitted into evidence. This is so the sanctity of the marital relationship will not be violated."

My mother seemed to like this explanation, as she had held her tongue and tolerated my father for thirty-five years, and presented a wan smile.

"In addition," my father continued, "the English common law, which is recognized to a large degree by most of the states, also prevents spouses from testifying against one another in a criminal proceeding. The rationale for this is the same."

It was my turn to interrupt. "Mom, the prosecution can object if I try to bring up what Jerry said to his wife, and Jerry can prevent her from testifying for the defense."

A flash of clarity appeared to form in my mother's eyes. "But didn't you say they had to be private conversations? I mean, Mrs. Lathrop told the cops about what was said between her and her husband. Somehow doesn't that act as a waiver of the privilege?"

My father and I looked at each other dumbfounded. I suddenly realized mother had absorbed far more than I had imagined over the course of her life with a lawyer husband and son.

I continued. "Exactly right, mom. That's what I'll be arguing. She blew the marital privilege when she told the cops about it. But there's more. The law that establishes the marital conversation privilege has some exceptions. There is no privilege in a criminal proceeding in which one spouse is charged with a crime committed against the other spouse, or a child of either."

"Hmm," she intoned. "But in your case Sammy, the dad hasn't been *charged* with the crime. Won't that hurt you?"

Mom's perceptiveness amazed me. I could tell dad was anxious to intervene.

"Well, honey," he started, more condescendingly than I would have liked, "there's the law that's in the books. Then there's the law between the judge's ears. Most good judges, if they get any decent evidence that someone else may have committed the crime, will lean overboard to allow evidence that points in that direction."

"I agree," I said. "But then there's the testimonial privilege that bars testimony against a spouse in a criminal proceeding. I can't argue that the conversation should come in because Lathrop committed the crime, and then say it's not a criminal trial because he hasn't been charged."

"It does get pretty confusing," my mother said.

"Yes, it does." Dad took a long draught of his pinot, seemingly to get maximum effect on what was to follow. "That last one is your primary problem. You can be sure Mr. Lathrop will insist on the privilege, and I can't see any judge not enforcing it."

The rest of the evening was spent in discussions about my sister, Mary, whom I hadn't seen in a couple of years. She was married with two kids, and my parents were infatuated with their grandchildren. It seemed to me they made a point of drawing comparisons between my bachelor lifestyle and the familial bliss of my sister's. My parents left the next day, to our mutual relief.

I didn't bring up my other major legal hurdle—convincing the judge to allow me to introduce into evidence Lathrop's sperm sample and the test results based on that sample. There's this thing in the law called "chain of custody." If you seek to get a substance before a jury that may have passed through a few hands, or a mouth as in my case, you must demonstrate that the item remained the same throughout the journey.

For the police, it's simple—a cop, whether it be a uniform or technical, testifies he found an object at a crime scene, transported it in a sealed evidence bag to a locker or lab, then retrieved it to bring it to

Selfie

court. My chain of custody depended on Janine and Dr. Gordon. The weak link was Janine. If I lost her testimony, for any reason, as to how she acquired and stored Lathrop's semen, I could never get Gordon's lab results into evidence. I had to pray the State wouldn't put two and two together, and realize Janine's importance to the case. I knew if Lathrop became aware of who she was, and what she was up to, her life would be in danger.

I spoke with her about my fears one evening at home several days later while we were enjoying a glass of chardonnay and some Led Zeppelin on the stereo.

"Hey honey, gotta' talk to you about something," I opened.

She had pulled a bud of grass from a tiny pillbox and was making a valiant effort to light it in a pipe. The bud appeared green and wet, and it took a lot of sucking for her to cajole a sullen cloud of dark smoke from it.

"What's up, sweetie?" she sputtered.

"Need to talk to you about the trial. You know that if Lathrop connects you to the semen sample, he'll do everything in his power to keep you from testifying. I don't want you to be in any danger."

"I'll be okay."

"You may not be, and I can't take that chance. You're not dealing with Lathrop alone—he's got a few other cops with him that we need to look out for."

"Babe, they don't scare me."

"Well, they scare me. Is there a place you can go to, quickly, if I find they've connected you to the case? Like your mom's?"

I knew Janine's folks were divorced, her father was of parts unknown, and her mother still lived in the Bay area.

"Do you think that would ever be necessary?" She had put down the pipe, still out of breath.

"It would give me some peace of mind. Especially immediately after you've testified. That's the most dangerous time."

"Okay, I'll call her. She only has a one bedroom, but I'm sure she'd make the pull-out sofa available to me."

"Great."

Chapter Twenty-four

Our opportunity to discuss the matter with Janine's mom, Alice, came sooner than we thought.

Hurricanes in Key West are the tornadoes, wild fires, and floods found in the rest of the country. A lot of people ask me, how can you live with all the hurricanes, and I respond, I'd rather have a natural disaster that gives me three to five days advanced warning, than one that can wipe me and my friends out in an instant. Plus, we haven't had a direct strike in Key West in over ten years. Yes, we ordinarily get them every three to five years, but they're usually minor. The last major hurricane was Wilma in 2005. We've all heard of the Labor Day hurricane of 1935, which, although not rated then, we know now was a category five hurricane. It's the one that totally destroyed the Flagler railroad that had operated continuously since 1912.

Four days after my tête-a-tête with Janine, the National Weather Service announced that Hurricane Gustav had formed in the Caribbean and was tracked to at least graze the Lower Key. We discussed the situation and decided it might be a good opportunity to travel to California where I could meet Alice and we could ask her if

Janine could stay with her on a moment's notice.

It cost us a fortune, as we had to make the reservations only two days before our scheduled departure, and put the pets in the kennel on Stock Island which was hurricane protected, but it was worth it. The day before our flight we put up all the hurricane shutters and removed all loose lawn furniture or anything else that might fly around, and crammed it into my small garage adjoining the house.

We took the shuttle to Miami and a direct flight to San Francisco. On the way, we had a couple of Proseccos and talked.

"How do you think it's going, I mean, us living together?" she asked.

"I think very well. In fact, better than I expected."

"Me, too. In fact, you're my best friend in Key West."

"A BFWB, huh?"

I was surprised to see a look of confusion on her face, but she quickly recovered. "Yes, that too."

I leaned closer to her and offered my glass for a toast, which she clinked, saying, "Skoal."

"Now that I think about it," I said, "I have to agree. You've become my friend, confidante, and of course my lover. I really appreciate you, honey."

"The feelings are mutual." She gave me a wet kiss on my cheek.

We spent the first night at the airport Hilton—I found out on the trip that her mother did not drive—and rented a car and caught some sights the next morning: Golden Gate Bridge, Fisherman's Wharf,

Union Square. Having been cloistered on a small island for the past several years, I was impressed with the vibrancy and sophistication of this marvelous city. We also booked a room at a small B & B in the vicinity where her mom resided.

We arrived at Alice's duplex on Jackson Street in the Presidio Heights area of the City around two in the afternoon. Janine told me her mother had rented the same one-bedroom rent-controlled unit for over twenty years, and paid seven hundred and fifty dollars a month, about one-fifth of the current going rate.

It was a very pleasant area of town, a quiet, tree-lined street with well kept-up properties. Alice was at the door when we arrived. I had seen one photo of her, taken when she was in her early twenties, just a year before she had Janine. It was taken at the Monterrey Pop Festival in 1969. In the shot, she was in typical flower child costume—long, granny dress, flowers in her hair, even John Lennon spectacles perched low on her nose.

Time had treated Alice gently. There was little change from that Festival photo. Sure, more lines in her brow, a general graying of the hair, but still quite cute and vivacious. Janine and her mom could have been separated at birth.

Her unit was small but well-organized. Janine had told me Alice had worked as a teller at the local bank for over fifteen years. We decided to have lunch in Chinatown, a long but pleasant walk. I had been to the Chinese districts in New York and Boston, but those paled in comparison to San Fran. This area was enormous with restaurants five to a block. Alice had her favorite, and we went there. Over Moo Goo Gai Pan and King Tso Chicken, we got to know each other.

"So," Alice started, "Janine tells me you're a lawyer."

"Yep, about ten years now."

"Have you always practiced in Key West?"

I explained to her the path that had led me there, and said, "Key West's unique in every way. I've never experienced any place like it. A real atmosphere of acceptance—no one cares what you look like, what your preferences are—so long as you don't hurt anyone else."

"This city is a lot like that too. We have a huge LBGT community here."

"I know you do, and I'm very impressed with your beautiful city. I'd consider moving here, except I've gotten very used to the slow, laid-back pace of the islands."

"I hope to visit some time."

"We'd love it if you did."

Janine's sharp glance told me she hadn't broken the news we were living together.

"What kinds of cases do you do?"

"Mostly criminal, some personal injury, domestic relations. Frankly, whatever comes in the door with Mr. Green."

Alice looked nonplussed.

"Sorry. That's a trade expression for someone with money."

"Oh."

"What about you?" I asked. "Janine's told me some things, but how's your job going?"

I had opened the floodgates. I got the impression Alice didn't have many people to talk to. She started by telling me she had grown up in the Modesto, California area—her dad had been in the vanguard of the technology industry with IBM, then Hewlett-Packard. She attended the University of California at Berkeley, but never graduated.

There she met Janine's father—whom she consistently referred to as "the asshole" without any correction from Janine—and the marriage lasted five years. Raised Janine alone and never remarried. My general impression was that Alice was a simple, kind person who possibly had smoked a little too much gange or dropped more than her fair share of acid back in the day.

We finished our meal and I suggested the two of them head off and spend some time alone while I wandered the city. We agreed to get together at Alice's for dinner that early evening. I took the ferry to Alcatraz—I had always been fascinated with the old prison. I wandered the decrepit cell blocks, looked at the writing carved into the concrete and metal bars. What horror, loneliness did they describe in this rancid, dank hell-hole? All I knew was that I would do anything to keep Bob from wasting away in prison for the remainder of his life.

When we arrived back at the dock, I stopped to take a photo of it. I saw a man in my line of sight turn around suddenly and pull the baseball cap he was wearing lower over his eyes. The precipitous action disturbed me, so I aimed my cell phone and clicked. There was something about him—his gait, the way his shoulders slightly drooped, that seemed familiar.

I studied the photograph after he had walked away. Was it Officer Shields of the Key West Police Department? I couldn't quite tell but it sure looked like him. He had been involved in at least a half-dozen cases of mine. And what was he doing in San Francisco, within spitting distance of me? It was an unsettling thought, but I dismissed it because I was not positive it was him.

When I arrived at Alice's, it was obvious the two were well into their cups. They also, as I saw now, had a close, loving relationship. Alice had prepared a sumptuous salad, which included arugula, grape tomatoes that she had grown in her tiny backyard garden, and walnuts and cranberries. There was also a delightful selection of various kinds of sushi.

It seemed that Janine and Alice had discussed what we had come there to broach with Alice. Alice said, as we were capping the meal with a dessert wine I had picked up on my peregrinations around the city, "So Janine tells me you're handling a case involving a cop and the murder of his daughter."

"Yes. I can't tell you too much, but the dad is a loose cannon."

"Is Janine in any danger?" Alice's expression clearly indicated she was very worried.

"Not now. My only concern is that, when she testifies . . ." and I could tell by Alice's bemused expression that Janine had told her everything, ". . . "when she testifies the cops may seek some retribution."

"Are the cops in Key West really that bad?"

Selfie

"Certainly, not all of them. But they have a small pool of eligible candidates for the force down there, and a couple of them clearly fell through the cracks."

"That's terrible. I hated the cops in college, but I know now there are a lot of good ones, and our society would be lost without them."

"There are also a lot of great cops in Key West. We just got the dregs in this case. As with most rotten fruit, they spoil the rest. I do wish the good ones would better police their corrupt counterparts. The 'brotherhood' concept sometimes goes too far."

"What can *I* do?" Alice asked.

Janine answered. "Mom, I just may need to come out here immediately after my testimony. They don't know about you, our last names are now different, so I'm sure you'd be in no danger."

"Wel,l I'm going to do more than that," Alice said, and she excused herself from the table and headed into the bedroom.

Janine and I looked at each other in surprise. A minute later Alice came out wearing a shoulder holster with a .357 magnum inserted firmly into it. I was flabbergasted. Alice was the last person I would ever think would be carrying. Janine looked amused at my shock.

"Completely licensed, good in Florida. I can check it at the airport and pick it up upon arrival. I'll fly out to Key West just before the trial and stay until its conclusion. No way anyone's going to harm my baby."

I was completely taken aback. This remnant of the '60s was a pistol-packin' momma?

"I can't really let you do . . ."

Alice put a finger to her lips and shushed me. "Sorry Sam. There's no debate about this. I'm going."

And that's the way we left it.

Janine and I determined that Hurricane Gustav had headed out into the Gulf and posed no further danger to us.. We flew back, enjoying an overnight in South Beach.

We arrived back in Key West in the evening. I always loved coming into the Key West airport. It held itself out as in international airport, but was more like a third-world terminal. You entered and exited the plane on rolling stairs and walked across the tarmac. A mural, depicting a happy, multi-racial family welcoming all arrivals, was painted on the wall.

We took a cab to the house. As we approached the porch, I noticed a slight gap in the shutter protecting the front door. I knew I had latched it tight at the time of our departure. I pulled open the shutter and saw the door was ajar. I motioned for Janine to stop and I slowly opened the door and yelled loudly, "Is anyone in there?"

Janine whispered, "What is it?"

"Someone's been in here. Stay here and don't move."

There was no sense in calling the cops. It was them I feared had been in there. Thank God the lights worked. The living room was just as we had left it. But when I entered my bedroom, I could easily see someone had rifled through my belongings—bureau drawers were pulled out haphazardly, and some boxes I kept on the top shelf of the closet were scattered on the floor.

I heard Janine exclaim, "Oh God." I strode quickly to the doorway into her bedroom. She was standing there with her hand still over her mouth. Her room was in worse shape. Someone had ransacked it—clothes, shoes, papers and jewelry were strewn about. "Try to see if anything's missing, I said.

I returned to my room and began sorting out the mess. I could hear Janine rummaging through her room. After fifteen minutes, she came to my door and said, "All my jewelry's still here, so it couldn't have been a robbery." Looking further and checking more drawers, she came back and said, "Shit, Sam, my passport is missing."

"Are you sure?"

"Yeah, I'm sure."

"Why would they take that?"

"Because it says Janine Reynolds on it."

Chapter Twenty-Five

At my insistence, Janine called her mother the next day. Now that they knew who "Janine Reynolds" was, I had no doubt her life was in danger.

I agreed to foot the bill to have Alice fly to Key West as soon as she could. I was certain it was Officer Shields I had seen in San Francisco. It was evident he was "keeping the peek" and making sure I was not home while they broke into my home.

I also paid for a security company to alarm the house. It killed me to do it as I had always felt safe in my little home, and Key West is generally a very sheltered city to live in. I didn't know anyone who locked their doors during the day.

Alice arrived two days later with a trunk of clothes and her cat Santana. I guess similarities in cat-naming ran in the family. She also described to me how she could process her pistol through the various gate screenings. Janine and her mom had already agreed Alice would sleep with Janine in her bed. If three was a crowd among the two dogs and Jerry Garcia, the addition of Alice's feline was a riot. Santana was not allowed out the bedroom door by the resident, and now territorial pre-existing animals, so Alice had to place her cat's food, water, and litter box in their room. It turned out to be okay because Alice was assiduous in keeping everything spotless.

Alice easily adapted to Key West life, taking long walks along the shady streets of Old Town and the beaches. She also turned out to be an excellent cook, enjoyed the art and was very creative in her concoctions. Janine and I paid for the food and Alice walked daily to our nearby local market for that night's supper.

It was time, as Bob had said, to "get it on." I had re-interviewed all my prospective witnesses and filed my lists. I sat down and typed up a "Demand for Speedy Trial," which I promptly filed with the court with a copy to Dan.

I knew the Sixth Amendment to the United States Constitution guaranteed a criminal defendant the right to a speedy and public trial. That right is also codified in the Florida Statutes, section 3.197 to be exact. That law allows a defendant to file a "demand for a speedy trial." But you better be ready to go to trial when you submit it because the court can schedule trial within five to forty-five days after a hearing on the demand. Even without a formal demand, the law states that someone charged with a felony must be tried within sixty days, but that law is riddled with exceptions. In the real world, cases can linger for well over a year.

Defense attorneys rarely avail themselves of this option. That's because we know delay almost always inures to the benefit of the defendant. Usually, the prosecution has quickly and fully developed its case. That's because the state has all the resources. I liken the prosecution's case to a clear stream flowing to an inevitable guilty verdict, and it is our duty to sit on the banks of that stream and throw clods of mud into it. Obfuscation is the opiate of the defense bar. We know, despite the court's instructions to the jury on the presumption of innocence, most people feel that for an individual to have been dragged that far into the criminal justice system, they must be guilty of something. In essence, we have the burden of proving our guy's innocence,

I received notice the next day that the Judge wanted to see counsel in his chambers the following Wednesday, October 14. It was common for a judge to want a "lobby conference" before scheduling a trial to get an idea how many witnesses might *actually* testify—as opposed to what counsel had set forth in their lists—and what evidentiary issues might arise at trial.

Dan and I met with Judge Thorpe at nine sharp. The judge had removed his robe, and was in shirtsleeves and a tie. He was in a genial, but serious mood. "All right, gentlemen, we've got a nasty case before us now. I want any bickering between you kept to the minimum. I know there's a lot at stake here but don't let your zeal translate into rants against each other. Understood?"

Dan and I, somewhat reluctantly on my part, acknowledged our consent.

"I've got your lists here," he continued. "So, Mr. Thompson, let's start with you. Which of these on your witness list do you honestly intend to call?"

"All of them, Judge," he replied.

"C'mon, Mr. Thompson. You've got eighteen witnesses listed here, many of whom are law enforcement or first responders. I don't think you need to call everyone who was within two miles of the scene."

"I'll see what I can do to cut it down, Judge," Dan said sullenly.

Thorpe turned to me. "How about you Attorney Harris. Are you going to re-call everyone on Mr. Thompson's list?"

"No, Judge. If Dan calls them all, I certainly won't bore the jury with redundancy. I just didn't want to be caught with my pants down if he skipped over someone I thought the jury would want to hear from."

"I see," Judge Thorpe replied. "Now I understand the defendant's DNA was found on the murder weapon. Is that correct Mr. Thompson?"

"Yes, it was. And his fingerprints on the girl's bike."

"Damning evidence, no, Mr. Harris?"

I had to be very careful here. Not the time to reveal too much of my hand. "I hope to show there's another explanation for the prints being there."

Thorpe's prodigious eyebrows shot up. "Oh?"

"I'm not going to say too much about it right now, but there may have been some carelessness in the handling of evidence."

"The words of a desperate man, Judge," Dan said.

Judge Thorpe shot him a withering glance.

"We'll see about that," I replied.

Rusty Hodgdon

The judge called in his session clerk and we went over our respective calendars. We set the trial date for November 18, just a little more than a month away. I had never witnessed a murder trial come to this point so quickly—just six months since the crime. I had my work cut out for me.

Chapter Twenty-Six

As the trial date approached, I became more and more anxious. Sleep became sporadic. I started drinking more. I called Ben and invited him over for a cold one at Louie's. When we had ordered, and sat down, his first comment opened the door to what I wanted to discuss with him.

"Great Jehovah," he said, "you look like crap. Are you ill?"

"No, but this case is weighing heavily on me. Frankly Ben, I'm scared shitless. If Bob is convicted and gets life, I could never forgive myself."

"It's always tougher representing an innocent man than a guilty one."

"Yes, it is . . . assuming he's innocent."

"Are you starting to doubt that now?"

"No, not really . . . but maybe. I mean there's so much evidence against him. I just can't seem to get my head around the fingerprints on the bike. Why didn't he ever mention that to me?"

"Cause the way you describe him he's always a day late and a dollar short...especially on the mental side of things."

"Okay, I guess you're right."

"But c'mon Sam. You know that's not the way to approach a case. You can't worry about the outcome or whether your client is guilty or innocent—you can only be concerned about the process—doing the damndest for your client."

"I know, I know. But this is different. I like Bob. I would never have become involved if Judge Thorpe hadn't appointed me."

"Well, he did, and you have to suck it up and face it. And stop drinking, goddamn it. You look terrible."

"You're right, Ben. I've got to find a way to deal with this pressure other than drowning myself in alcohol."

"Tell you what, Sam. I've always found a good way to focus on the solution rather than the fear, is to outline the case. You know, the pro's and con's. Here, let's make a list of the strengths and weaknesses of your defense."

Ben pulled a large napkin out of a holder on the table and a gold Cross pen out of his lapel pocket. I couldn't remember the last time I had seen a Cross pen.

"Okay, let's do the con's first. Help me out here."

"Okay."

He wrote *cons* on the left side of the napkin. "We've got the fact that your guy was in the vicinity of the crime at or about the time it was perpetrated." He wrote *at scene of crime* on the napkin.

"Yep, that's what led to his interrogation," I said.

Selfie

"Second, his fingerprints were found on the young girl's bike." He scribbled *fingerprints on bike* in the same column.

"Yes, but we've got an answer for that."

"Hold on Sam. This is the 'con' list. Next we've got Bob's DNA on one of the pieces of wood."

I held my tongue as the photos of the cops putting the two pieces of wood in the same evidence bag came to mind.

He put *defendant's DNA on murder weapon* on the paper.

"Lastly, we've got the snitch who's going to say Bob told him he killed the girl."

"Yeah, that lying bastard," and *snitch's testimony* was added to the list. I looked at the napkin, which read:

Cons

~At scene of crime

~Fingerprints on bike

~Defendant's DNA on Murder weapon

~Snitch's testimony

It wasn't the boost I was looking for. In fact, it was damning. I took a long swig off my Captain Morgan.

"Okay, now to the pro's," Ben continued. "I'm going to leave out for the time being the DNA evidence linking Jerry Lathrop and at least one other to the murder. "First, we've got the selfies seemingly showing someone carrying a lifeless young girl to the edge of the Salt Ponds, with Bob and Harley in the foreground." He wrote selfie photos in the pro column.

I knew there were problems with the photos. Dan would have a field day pointing out the graininess and distance of the shot from the action.

"Then there's the testimony of Sally that Jerry liked her to dress up as a little school girl, and that he told her his child looked beautiful naked."

I didn't say it, but I knew there'd be a battle over the admissibility of those statements. It was crass hearsay, that is, testimony in-court as to what someone said out-of-court, but I planned to argue that it was a statement against penal interest, an exception to the hearsay rule. The law provides that if someone says something that could arguably expose them to criminal liability, that statement is sufficiently reliable to be repeated in court by another.

Ben kept at it. He wrote Lathrop statement about nude daughter in the pro column.

"Then there's the testimony of the wife that her husband went

Selfie

out to look for Frances around the time of her murder and came back with changed clothing."

"Yeah, but . . ."

"Stop," Ben said sternly. "We're being optimistic in our pro category. We'll get that in." He wrote *wife's testimony about looking for Frances.*

I was not nearly as sanguine about those prospects. The cops couldn't testify to what Betty Lathrop had told them, again, because it was hearsay, and the marital privilege was about as strong a privilege as there is in the law. But I suddenly realized what he had said.

"We're…we'll, Ben? What do you mean by that?"

"Because young man, I'm sitting second seat at the trial. Meet your new co-counsel." He grabbed my hand and shook it.

"Ben, you know I can't pay you out of my own pocket, and the funds from the State have been over-spent. And it's too late to get a motion in front of Judge Thorpe to have you appointed so the State of Florida could pay you.."

"Don't you worry about all of that. I won't charge you a penny. Hey, this could be fun."

"I don't know how to thank you." I felt as if a huge weight had been lifted from my shoulders. To have an experienced and extremely intelligent lawyer next to me throughout the trial would be a godsend.

"No problem. Now let's get back to work." Ben spread the napkin out on the table.

"Oh, we forgot about Lathrop's DNA on his daughter's shorts." I sensed it was not critical evidence, as they were household members.

Ben added that to the napkin. It now read as follows:

Cons	Pros
~At scene of crime	~Selfie photos
~Fingerprints on bike	~Lathrop's statement about nude daughter
~Defendant's DNA on Murder weapon	~Wife's testimony about looking for Frances
~Snitch's testimony	~Lathrop DNA on Frances' shorts

"Honestly Sam, based on a general analysis of the pro's and con's of the case, there's no question you must convince the jury that Jerry Lathrop killed his daughter. It's crucial."

"I realize that. And that puts Janine directly in the cross-hairs."

"Yes, it does."

Chapter Twenty-Seven

Fantasy Fest in Key West was just two weeks away. It's the Mardi Gras of the city, when bad behavior and nudity are tolerated for an entire week. A "zone" is established, about twelve square blocks, where scanty clothing, bare breasts minimally disguised by body painting, and public drunkenness are allowed.

This year's theme was "Harlots and Harlequins." All day and night the bars and restaurants held special events, with titles such as: the "Luv2Glow" party; the "Anything but Clothes" event; "Boxers or Briefs;" Gangsters and Molls; Halos and Horns" pool party and wet t-shirt contest; "Dirty doctors and Nurses." You get my drift.

I had never been interested in the Fest until I met Janine. She loved to dress in costume. She always managed to turn her substantial breasts into an eye-popping illusion with the creative use of body paint.

It was a bacchanalia of week-long proportions. My favorite was the Masquerade March, also known as the "locals parade." It started on Frances Street next to the cemetery and split into two groups, one headed north, the other south. The date was October 29—Friday night.

Rusty Hodgdon

Janine dressed on the harlot side—a short-short tutu with tiny red lace panties on full display. I was a rather fierce-looking clown patterned after Emmett Kelly—with a mean streak. Alice wisely chose to stay home.

The costumes in the parade are mostly homegrown and incredibly creative. As you strolled along old town's small streets, the residences and small businesses set up tables along the route serving free jello shots and other libations.

There was, as usual, a strong police presence. Not obtrusive, but noticeable. As we rounded the corner of Fleming and Simonton Streets, I saw Stearn speaking with another officer off to the right. I tried to pull Janine by the arm to the left, but it was too crowded to get more than a few feet toward the center.

As far as I was concerned, Janine and I were unrecognizable in our costumes. Our friends said as much. I was shocked when Stern made his way quickly toward us and grabbed Janine harshly by the elbow and said "Lady, we don't allow public nudity." He began to pull her to the side of the street. My first thought was that he had seen us exit my house in costume, or worse, watched as we donned and prepared our costumes in the house.

I didn't think—I just reacted. I encircled my arms tightly around Janine's waist and pulled in the opposite direction. When I saw this was causing her pain, I quickly let go and strode directly into Stern's path. He bumped me, chest to chest, and said, "OK, Attorney Harris. If that's the way you want it, you're under arrest for interfering with a law enforcement officer in the conduct of his official business."

I didn't budge, and gave him the nastiest look I could muster. It was time to stand my ground with this bastard. Thankfully another officer with whom I had been friendly for several years joined us and whispered in Stearn's ear. He nodded, let go of Janine's elbow, and walked away. It was then I saw the chief come over. "Do we have a problem, Mr. Harris?"

"No problem, chief, so long as you get your troops on their leashes."

He gave me a frown, and proceeded back to where he had been standing.

That ruined the night for us. Janine had three dark bruises on her biceps where Stern's meaty fingers had dug in. We went home and downed the two bottles of champagne we had kept ready to celebrate later that night.

****

It started when I found Harley by the birdbath in the southeast corner of my backyard. He was panting laboriously and huge chunks of saliva were bubbling up from his nostrils. Jessie had been acting aloof all morning. When I tried to coax him inside with a chunk of hamburger meat, he didn't budge. I brought his water bowl and placed it next to his head, which hung languidly to the side as he lay there. He lapped haphazardly.

I gave it an hour, and when I saw no improvement, I rushed him to the vets on Stock Island. Dr. Waters blasted him with vitamins and fluids for several hours while I waited in the reception area. Ultimately, she came to the door leading from the back. I didn't like the expression on her face—at all. It was a mixture of sorrow and professional fortitude that didn't bode well. "Sam," she said, "did you notice Harley eating anything unusual in the yard—I mean, like rotten food, or anything like that?"

"I found him with a bone, out in the backyard, earlier. I didn't recognize it so I took it away from him threw it in the trash."

"We'll start there. Do you think you could find it?"

"I'll try. Do you want me to and bring it to you if I do find it?"

"Please."

I went home, rousted around in the garbage, and found it among some decaying eggshells and a rotten pineapple I had thrown away. I drove directly back. Dr. Waters told me she'd send it to the lab and get back to me.

Early the next morning I received a call from the receptionist asking me to come right down to the animal hospital. Dr. Waters was waiting for me. "Sam, I've got bad news. That bone you gave me was doused with rat poison. Harley is in terrible pain. There's no hope here. We've got to put him down."

Selfie

I sat down in the closest chair. I couldn't believe it. "Are you sure?"

"I am. We could probably keep him alive for a few more days, but it would only prolong the agony. I wouldn't put anyone or anything through that."

I nodded my head and she motioned me into one of the examination rooms. Harley was spread out on the table, IVs protruding from several areas of his body. She asked me if I was ready.

I held Harley's large head in the crook of my arm. He was barely breathing. Dr. Waters attached a new vial to the IV. In less than two minutes I felt Harley flinch, and then his labored breathing stopped. I thanked the doctor, and she told me she'd send me a bill. I went out to my car and bawled like I had never bawled before, and pounded the steering wheel with my fist, badly bruising my right hand.

I knew what had happened, those bastards. I blamed myself. Harley died because of me. It could have just as easily been Jessica. I had no idea how I was going to tell Bob about this. I decided to wait until after the trial.

I never received that bill.

Chapter Twenty-Eight

Trial was now a month away. There's always a meeting a defense counsel has with his client prior to a criminal proceeding. It's about the defendant testifying at trial. Most defendants say they want to testify, more I've always felt because of a need to show some bravado in the face of their usually overwhelming guilt. Defense counsel will almost always urge their clients not to testify, knowing that in the vast majority of cases they will inevitably stick both feet firmly inside their mouths, or elsewhere.

My fears about Bob testifying were stronger than the norm—he got confused easily and his testimony would place him at the scene of the crime. But knowing Bob, I was sure he would insist on it.

I made another trip to the jail. The early November sky was a baby blue with temperatures in the seventies. We don't have the phantasmagoric colors of a New England Fall, but we do have the cleanest salt ocean air and emerald water anywhere. Bob looked more apprehensive than I had ever seen him. He also had a large bandage over his right eye.

"What happened to you?" I asked.

His brow was knit and his lower lip quivered as he spoke.

"I was in the small exercise corridor where we PC's are allowed to roam. After a few minutes, I noticed the entrance door was ajar—the one I had just gone through and knew I had closed—and three guys who are the toughest bastards in this joint walked in. They had to have been let in by a guard. I fought them off as best I could," and with this Bob raised his two hands up and made fists. His knuckles were badly bruised and scarred.

"Jesus," I said. "What happened?"

Again, that smirk from Bob. "I knocked the living crap out of them. But if they'd had shivs, my ass would have been grass. Finally, a screw came and got them, only because I think he was afraid for their safety. I think it's only a matter of time before they get to me armed."

"Do you know the names of the inmates, or the guard?"

"They call the guard 'Sully.' I think his last name is Sullivan. No clue who the inmates are, except for their gang names—one is 'Tat,' another 'Monkey.' Don't know the third. But maybe you shouldn't say anything. I haven't. I told the infirmary folks I had tripped and fallen."

"Are you kidding? I've got to say something. You could've been killed."

"Maybe that would be for the best. I can't spend the rest of my life in prison."

"I'm going to do my best to keep that from happening."

I figured it was time to tell Bob about the evidence against Lathrop. "I haven't intentionally withheld anything from you. I just wasn't confident enough about this part of our defense until recently."

"What's that Sam?"

"We've got evidence Jerry Lathrop is the one who killed his daughter." I decided not to mention Stearn at this time for fear I'd confuse Bob with sensory overload.

"What? How is that possible?"

"We were able to retrieve your recent photos from your iCloud account, including the selfies around the Salt Ponds on the day of the murder."

"You got my photos? Really? That's fantastic." Bob was almost crying.

"Yes, all of them. Several of them show you and Harley, but something else in the background."

"What Sam? What?" He was shouting now.

"They're very grainy and difficult to see in detail, but I believe they show Jerry Lathrop carrying his comatose, or dead daughter, to the edge of the water."

Bob stood bolt upright. "Then I'll get off, right? I'll be found not guilty?"

"It's great evidence, but please, don't assume anything."

Now he looked despondent, and sat down heavily.

"But we have more. We may be able to put into evidence that the father was mad at his daughter for not coming home in time, went out looking for her, and returned in a full change of clothing without her. All at or around the time she was killed."

Bob leapt to his feet again. I felt my neck rebel against the sudden upward movement to keep my eyes on him.

"My God, Sammy. This is sounding better and better."

"Again, Bob, there're difficulties in trying to get some of this into evidence."

"Like what?"

I explained in the best non-legal terms I could about the marital privilege. I continued, "It doesn't end there, Bob. We think we've found Jerry's DNA at the crime scene—in addition to the DNA of another, unknown person."

With that Bob put his head in his hands and started sobbing uncontrollably. I was mildly embarrassed. "C'mon, Bob. It's good news."

"I know it is," he said between gasps. "It's just that I've been so worried. Before this, it seemed all the news was bad."

"I thought you needed to hear some good news for a change."

"I sure did."

I had never seen such an elated grin on Bob's face, even after winning a tough bocce game.

"There's another important issue I need to discuss with you. I think you know you can't be forced to testify at your trial, right?"

"Yeah, I know that."

"We need to discuss, at some point, not necessarily now, whether you'll testify or not."

"Wouldn't it be better to wait until after the prosecutor finishes his case to make that decision?" Bob asked.

I was astonished. Was this Bob speaking? "Why yes, it would. Uh, good point. In fact, I would say we can wait until the very end of our case. If a defendant is going to testify, it's best to have him do it last. But I should tell you that I rarely recommend that a client testify. Any little inconsistency, however trivial, can turn a case the wrong way."

"Sounds good," Bob said. "But can we practice beforehand so I'll be ready if I testify?"

"Yes. We'll start that in a day or two."

For the first time, I honestly considered having Bob testify in his own defense.

Chapter Twenty-Nine

Over the ensuing weeks, I met personally with each of my serious witnesses—those I was sure I would call to the stand: Sally, Janine, Ralph DePiero, Cody Thurber, Tyler, Dr. Gordon, and of course, Bob. I made two visits to Miami to meet with the Doctor. His testimony had to be simplified to the point where the average juror could fully understand it.

I met with him at his office on Collins Avenue at its intersection with 50th Street in Miami Beach. I realized I had not only never been to his office before, but I had never met him. It was on the fourth floor of a five story coral stone office building. The reception area was small but tidy. A pleasant, middle-aged and attractive woman led me to his office in the back corner of the building. I noticed several laboratories off to each side.

His office was of moderate size and I caught a fleeting glimpse of the baby blue ocean to the east. It looked organized, but I could see through a crack in a small room divider behind his desk a semblance of disorder—open books piled atop each other, stacks of papers in disarray.

Dr. Gordon walked around to the front of his desk to greet me. I was pleased to see he was handsome in a rugged, Harrison Ford way, and was professionally attired in a spotless, white lab coat with a blue, button-down shirt and striped red and black tie. We spoke briefly about the weather and the Florida Marlins, a team I could tell he did not suffer gladly, and then got down to business. He handed me a notebook that I found contained an exhaustive set of suggested questions, followed by his proposed answers, relevant to our case. I had never experienced such preparation by one of my expert witnesses.

"I usually find that it saves both of us a great deal of time if I prepare a direct examination appropriate to any case I'm involved in," he said in the deep baritone voice I had come to know. "You can make any changes you want. I see this as a beginning, not a final edition."

We went over them and I was amazed and deeply satisfied to see the attention to detail and organization of the materials. He also showed me some charts and graphs he had put together to augment his testimony. They were professionally prepared and easy to understand. I realized I had hit the jackpot with Dr. Gordon.

With the other witnesses, I ran through mock cross-examinations, peppering them with every conceivable leading question I thought the prosecutor might throw their way. Specifically, I admonished them to tell the truth, no matter what.

During the several days before the scheduled trial date, I stayed in touch with Judge Thorpe's session clerk, who was with him each day in court. Trials can be postponed simply because the judge is already engaged in a proceeding that extends longer than predicted. The day before our trial was to commence, I was told it was a green light. We'd start at nine the next morning, on November 18.

Chapter Thirty

Most lawyers, if their clients have the dough or they can get it from the court, will hire jury experts—those who will assist in the selection of the jury. I've never done it, even those few times when I had sufficient funds to do so. My feeling is that such so-called expertise is closer to black magic than it is scientific methodology. If I couldn't, together with the collective years of wisdom that Ben had accumulated, pick a better jury for my client than those who had never argued a case in a court of law, I might as well tear down and trash my shingle. The OJ Simpson trial was a case in point. It took hundreds of thousands of dollars in fees to conclude black people would be the best jurors. I could have done that for much less.

In a criminal case, there is no political correctness. Even though the courts have frowned upon attempts to exclude jurors based on race, religion or national origin, lawyers regularly do it—but very carefully. You pick the juror you think will most likely return a not guilty verdict. There are races, cultures and nationalities that lawyers learn are more lenient on criminal defendants, and we will pick those with only a fleeting thought about profiling. We always look for the misfit, the renegade, that person who will not swallow the government's story, hook, line and sinker. In general, black people fit that bill, whether the defendant is white or black. Also, Hispanics. They have learned a distrust of the American government and its institutions, especially the judicial system. I also favor hippies and noticeable druggies. There's a lot of dope in Key West—and a lot of dopes. Anyone who has run up against the law and acquired a fear and dislike of the cops is a good candidate for my ideal juror.

Obviously, Ben and I avoided anyone who worked for the government, especially law enforcement, or who had relatives or family members in such capacities. Also, generally, we avoided women, especially in a rape case such as this. You ask any woman what they'd like to do to the rapist of a child and it would have something to do with a scrotum and a dull knife. For them, it doesn't matter who, just someone must pay.

In a normal criminal trial, the defense is entitled to an unlimited number of challenges based on certain criteria set forth by law, called "for cause" challenges. Close affiliation with the police or a clearly stated bias against those charged with a crime would obviously trigger such an objection to sitting a juror. On the other hand, in a non-capital case, that is, where the charges cannot result in the death penalty or life imprisonment, both sides are entitled to six challenges for any reason whatsoever, called peremptory challenges. Ethnic challenges would fit into that category.

But in a capital case, such as Bob's, we were entitled to a total of ten peremptory challenges each, which meant the state had to summons a huge number of people for the jury pool. The courthouse was packed this day with such prospective jurors, but also the gawkers, hangers-on, and the bored, who have always attended public events relating to the determination of guilt or innocence, or the punishment of those charged with a crime.

The jurors were organized in groups, A through E, with approximately twenty jurors in each group. Groups A and B were first led into the courtroom and filled the front ten rows of Courtroom D in the Key West courthouse on Whitehead Street. The public took the remaining back five rows.

Both Ben and I, and the prosecution, had prepared an extensive list of questions to ask the jurors. We had to obtain the court's prior approval for each question and Judge Thorpe was quick to cull out any repetitive or unduly probing ones. Each juror was brought up to the "side bar," which is just the end of the judge's bench furthest away from the jury box. Both Dan and I would run through our questions with each juror and decide if we wanted to exercise a "for cause" or "peremptory" challenge. All objections for cause would have to be approved by the judge.

Before each objection, Ben and I would go back to counsel table and make a show of involving Bob in the discussion. Usually all we would talk about was the weather or some especially attractive woman in the pool. We also gave Bob a pad of paper and some pens and told him to write something, even if it was gibberish. This pointed out to the jury the seriousness with which Bob took the proceedings.

Selfie

We were at it three full days before a jury of twelve and four alternates were seated. The alternates would sit through the entire trial, but would not deliberate unless one of the regular jurors had to be excused somewhere along the way. Ben and I were reasonably satisfied with our jury. It consisted of nine men and seven women, three of whom were black and two were Hispanic.

Chapter Thirty-One

During jury selection, it was Ben, Bob and myself at the defendant's table. On the prosecution side, Dan started with a young assistant, a gorgeous female named Bridget. I knew she had to have graduated from law school, but she looked about twenty to me. The obvious chemistry between them made me think their relationship transcended the professional. I also recognized that the prosecution in a rape case would usually include a woman on its team to cover the examination of a witness on matters that involved some sensitive gender-related issues. She might also help sway a middle-aged male juror who was on the fence when it came time for deliberations. Our final jury was seated late in the afternoon, so the judge called a recess until the next morning to commence opening statements.

The prosecution always opened first, and gave their closing argument last. That next day I wasn't surprised to see a bevy of police officers, all decked out in their dress blues, fill the front two rows behind Dan. An obvious show of support for the dad. Jerry, as was true for all the potential witnesses, was sequestered and could not be in the courtroom until he testified for fear he, or any other witness for that matter, might tailor their words to be consistent with others.

Now opening statements, as the judge told the jurors after they had found their seats by 9:15, were not evidentiary in nature, but only served as an outline of what each side intended to prove. I knew Dan's techniques, and I knew he was going to be a total asshole. I rarely object during an opposing counsel's opening, but Dan so quickly launched into a personal diatribe against Bob, at one point swirling around, stabbing his finger at him and calling him a treacherous rapist and murderer, I stood and asked the judge for relief. He gave it to me, admonishing Dan to stick to the facts. Dan acted sheepish and contrite but I knew full well he thought he had accomplished his intended effect. The jury glared at Bob.

I prefer to present my opening immediately after the prosecution, especially as in this case where I felt the jury was unduly affected by the emotional presentation by the State. I could not do so in this instance—I didn't want to disclose my true defense until the prosecution had rested, and there was still no final decision on whether Bob would testify. *Our* opening statement must come immediately before our defense. But when Judge Thorpe asked if I wanted to open after Dan, I took the opportunity, while looking directly at the jury, to say, "No, Your Honor, I'm sure this jury will not be bamboozled by the prosecution's excessive emotion and verbiage, so I will wait for our case to commence to reveal the real facts in this case."

"Very well," Judge Thorpe said, and Dan stood and called his first witness.

Chapter Thirty-Two

Three days after my last jailhouse conversation with Bob, and two weeks before the trial, I had received an updated witness list from Dan. It contained one new name, Officer Robert Hutchins. I had no record of him being involved in the case. I immediately tried to contact him, leaving several messages at the police station for him to call me. I wasn't surprised when I heard nothing. Just before trial, after a little asking around, I found out Hutchins wasn't a police officer, but a corrections officer. I tried calling the jail, and finally went down there to look for him. I was informed he had left the jail and was working "somewhere out-of-state." I had a bad feeling about it.

Sure enough, Dan said, "The State calls Robert Hutchins."

I saw a young, twentyish man stand in the second row behind the prosecution table and begin to approach the witness stand. He looked like he had been directly pulled from the set of Top Gun—close cropped hair, chiseled chin, and clear blue eyes. He was in a police uniform I could not identify. I had no clue what I was going to say, but I felt in my gut I had to interrupt what was happening, even for a moment.

"Objection, Your Honor," I said and I struck the arm of my chair sharply as I stood to give emphasis to my words.

As they say in the law, if you have the facts on your side, pound the facts; if it's the law, pound the law, and it it's neither, pound the table.

Judge Thorpe appeared startled, and said in a somewhat surly tone, "What *is* the nature of your objection, Attorney Harris?"

"Your Honor, I was just given Mr. Hutchins' name several weeks ago, and all of my efforts to contact him have been met with stonewalling and outright trickery."

Dan said, "Judge, he was included in a revised witness list on September 20, the list was given to Mr. Harris on that date, and I know of no efforts by Mr. Harris to contact this witness."

I started to open my mouth when the Judge said in a loud voice, "Counsel. Side bar, now."

Dan and I preceded to the far corner of the bench away from the jury. Judge Thorpe asked the clerk for a copy of the prosecution's witness list. He reviewed it, and when he saw Hutchins' name, said, "Attorney Harris, his name is right here," and he leaned over with the list in his hand and finger next to the name. "The list is also dated almost a month prior."

"I know judge, but I called the police department multiple times, was always told he wasn't in, and then I found he was a Corrections Officer with the jail. I went over there personally and was told he no longer worked there, and they didn't know where he had gone."

"Did you ask Mr. Thompson where he was?"

It had never crossed my mind to ask Dan that question, because I knew it would be a futile effort. "No, Your Honor," and I knew that was the death knell of my objection.

"Well, Attorney Harris, you should have, and neither of you has complete control over your witnesses or their whereabouts. The objection is overruled, and Mr. Thompson, you may proceed."

Dan glanced over at the jury with an insipid, victorious grin on his face, while I tried not to look like I was slinking back to my chair.

When I got back to counsel table, Bob leaned over and whispered, "What is this all about? I know that guy from the prison."

"I don't exactly know, but I fear the worst."

Dan led Mr. Hutchins through the preliminary questions—name, address, where he was presently employed, which turned out to be the Jacksonville Police Department. Then he asked, "Drawing your attention to October 2, were you employed on that date?"

"Yes, I was."

"Where were you employed?"

"The Monroe County Department of Correction on Stock Island."

"What was your position there?"

"I was a Corrections Officer."

I could tell by Hutchins' short, concise answers that he was an experienced witness who was well-coached to answer the question, and only the question.

Selfie

"How long had you served in that capacity, Officer?"

"Two years."

"Now again referring to the date of October 2, were you on duty that day?"

"Yes, I was."

"At 3:10 p.m., where were you stationed?"

"In the visiting area."

Now it came to me. Who he was and why he was here. To relate Bob's loud-mouthed response to my revelation of the fingerprint and snitch evidence. Jesus Lord Almighty.

"Did something occur on that date?"

"Yes."

"What was that?"

"I was standing just outside one of the areas set off from the visiting area by room dividers where attorneys meet with their clients."

"Did you overhear a conversation in that room?"

I jumped to my feet and shouted way too loudly for the circumstances, "Objection, Your Honor." The jury noticeably jumped in unison in their seats.

Judge Thorpe growled at me, "Attorney Harris, you don't need to raise your voice in *my* courtroom."

"I'm sorry Your Honor, but I wanted to make sure this witness did not testify to what are clearly privileged conversations protected by the attorney-client privilege."

"Side bar, counsel."

When we had congregated at the corner of the dais, the judge asked Dan what evidence he intended to elicit through this witness. Dan explained exactly what I feared, that Hutchins had overheard Bob state that he was guilty of killing Frances.

"What is your objection, Attorney Harris? If made in private, I would agree with you—the statements couldn't come in because of the privilege. But here your client waived the privilege by speaking loudly enough for others to hear."

"But judge, I'm sure this witness positioned himself just so he could eavesdrop on my privileged conversations with my client."

"I doubt that," Judge Thorpe said, "but Attorney Thompson, lay a foundation for why your witness was where he was."

"Fine judge," Dan said. He continued his questioning.

"Mr. Hutchins, let's go back a minute. Can you describe the visitation area?"

"Yes, I can. The area is a large single room, maybe sixty by forty feet. There are approximately twenty metal tables—similar to picnic tables with attached benches—where visitors meet with the inmates."

Hutchins looked at Dan to see if he should continue, and when Dan gave him a barely perceptible nod, he said, "In the back area of the room there are a series of partitions—they are soundproofed with carpet and stand eight feet tall—cordoning off separate spaces where attorneys can meet with their clients."

"Are there doors into those areas?"

"Yes, also carpeted and as tall as the partitions."

"Was it normal for officers to be stationed near this area?"

"Yes, there have been attacks against attorneys by inmates in the past. Most attorneys want us there," and he looked directly at me as he spoke.

I knew it happened, albeit rarely. There are some criminals who want to silence the messengers of bad tidings.

"Was it unusual for you to be close to the partitioned areas that day?"

"Not at all. There's always someone there."

"Was the door to the partition where you overheard a conversation closed?"

"Not entirely. There was about a two to three-inch crack in the door."

Dan looked at the judge. He motioned with his head that he was satisfied with the stage set by Dan.

"So, did you overhear a conversation coming from one of the partitions?"

I stood and said, "Objection. Same grounds as we discussed."

"Overruled."

Dan repeated his question. Hutchins said, "I was standing next to the partition to the far left as you enter the visiting area. I overheard a man say, 'I did it. I killed that young girl.'"

I looked at the jury. They were aghast. Dan had cleverly not mentioned this testimony in his opening, clearly wanting to gain maximum surprise effect, both with the jury and us.

"Did you recognize the voice?" Dan asked.

"Yes, I did. I knew the inmate well. It was Bob Wilson," and he pointed to Bob.

"Did you stay to see who exited the partitioned area?"

"I did, but I had also seen who had entered it. It was occupied by Mr. Harris and Mr. Wilson. Mr. Wilson left first, followed by his attorney shortly thereafter." Now he pointed at me.

I felt thirty-two eyes riveted on us.

"Are you sure those were the words you heard?"

"Positive. I'll never forget it. It's the first confession I've ever heard coming from that area."

I again objected vehemently, complaining about the witness's characterization of the words as a "confession." The judge agreed and asked the jury to ignore that part of the witness' testimony. In my view, there is no more futile an instruction in law than a judge asking a jury to strike testimony from their memory. If anything, it reinforced it.

Dan announced he was finished with the witness. I stood and spent some time eliciting the fact that Hutchins hadn't heard any conversation preceding or following the statement, and got him to admit the statement could have been taken out of context. But the damage was done. This jury was going to be hard to bring around to our side. A very bad start to any trial.

Chapter Thirty-Three

Dan proceeded with the bevy of EMT's, cops, and even firefighters who responded to the scene of Frances' death. None of them implicated Bob in the crime, so with each one I simply asked if they had seen Bob in the area when they were there, which I knew they had not. I was waiting for Robert Albury, the detective who had placed the two wooden sticks in the same evidence bag.

Albury was in his late thirties and Bahamian in origin. Albury was an established family name for some of the early settlors who came to Key West from the Bahamas. There's still an area in the City, just west of Whitehead Street, called Bahama Village, which is the home to many of those who first came over. He was a good looking black man who had an easy air about him. I also knew him to be an outstanding soul singer who routinely graced the stages of many of our bars with his deep, baritone voice. It was said he once traveled with the group that now tours as the Temptations. I liked the man, so I didn't necessarily relish what I had to do.

When he was called, Dan walked him through the basics, when he arrived, what he observed, what he did. When asked if he had seen the two pieces of wood and what he did with them, he said "put them in the evidence bag*s*."

Plural bags. I had my lead in. I knew he had only been a detective for two years, so when it was my turn to question him, I brought that fact out in several repetitive questions to hammer home his inexperience to the jury.

My questions about the gathering of the evidence went like this:

"Detective Albury, I believe you testified on direct examination by Mr. Thompson that you found the two sticks, labeled Exhibits Eighteen and Nineteen respectively, close to each other on the ground about four feet from the shore of the Salt Ponds, is that correct?"

"Yes, it is."

"Which one did you see first, Exhibit Eighteen or Nineteen?"

"I think it was Exhibit eighteen, but they were close to each other as I've said, so I may have seen them at about the same time."

"And you gathered them because they were close to the scene of the killing and one of them had what appeared to be blood and hair residue on it, correct?"

"Yes, and I had also noticed what I considered to be blunt force trauma to the child's head."

"Visually, however, the other piece did not seem to have any blood or hair on it, is that right?"

"Right, but I also observed some teeth marks on that one. I didn't know exactly what they were, so I collected it for testing."

"When you saw the blood and hair, can we assume you thought

it might be the murder weapon?"

"I thought it might be."

"It may have contained the DNA of not only the victim, but also the perpetrator, right?"

"Right, but I didn't know for sure."

"No, not for sure, but a good indication it might have, right?"

"Correct."

"A very important piece of evidence, right, one that would have to be handled *very* carefully?"

Albury hesitated here. He sensed I was heading somewhere, but didn't know quite where. "Well, yeah."

"Detective, have you ever heard of the term contamination regarding the collection and storing of evidence?"

"Certainly, but that never happened here."

I was getting to him. He was becoming defensive.

"Could you define contamination for us?"

"Well, yeah, sure. Contamination occurs when certain evidence comes too close to other evidence and what was on the one gets on the other. But as I said, that didn't occur in this case."

"You know Ralph DePiero, don't you?"

Albury was suspicious now. His guard was on high alert. "What does that got to do with all this?"

I glanced at the judge, and said, "I'll ask the questions, Detective. Please answer the question."

He also looked at Judge Thorpe, who gave him a stern *answer the frickin' question* stare.

"Yes, I know him. Everyone does. One of the best-known photographers in town."

I remembered a book Ralph had published entitled *Soul of Key West*, which beautifully covered the music scene in Key West and had prominently displayed Albury and his formidable talent.

"Do you believe Mr. DePiero to be a reliable and honest man?"

Dan rose and voiced an objection, complaining that I was venturing into irrelevant territory. I asked the Judge for several more questions to tie everything together, which he allowed with a brief, "But let's get on with this, Attorney Harris."

I asked the question again.

"Uh, I guess so," the witness answered.

"Did you see him at the crime scene that day?"

Albury looked confused. Then a flash of memory seemed to come upon him. "I believe I did. He's at many crime scenes. Does photography for the Citizen."

"Let me show you a series of photographs, Detective, that I represent to you were taken by Mr. DePiero that day and at the scene of Frances' death."

Dan rose again. "Judge, I have no idea what Attorney Harris is about to show the witness."

I looked over at the prosecution table. I had already seen the thick packet of my proposed exhibits that I had sent to Dan months before, sitting next to some of his boxes of materials. "Your Honor, if

Selfie

the prosecutor will simply look inside that envelope on his desk," and I pointed to the packet, "which I sent to him some time ago, he will find the photographs I intend to show the jury. They're towards the middle, and have the notation, "Defendant's Photos of the Crime Scene" on the back.

Dan appeared embarrassed that he had no clue what I was talking about. I now realized he had not taken the time to go through the materials one by one, only assuming, I imagined, they were his photographs sent right back to him. A critical error by any lawyer.

He started sorting through them, and turned all the photos over to look at their backs. When he saw those words, he turned them back over. The gradual realization of what he was looking at spread like a cancer across his face. I expected his outburst.

"Objection, Your Honor. I don't know what Attorney Harris is intending to show here, but it's not germane to these proceedings and highly prejudicial to the State."

His desperation was palpable, and I could see the judge felt it as well. Judge Thorpe simply asked, "Attorney Thompson, did you or did you not receive those photographs from the defense prior to the discovery deadline?"

"Uh, I guess I did, but he unfairly buried them in the middle of the package."

The judge looked amused. "You're not serious, are you, Attorney Thompson?"

Dan did not answer. His face was red and beads of sweat had

formed on his brow.

The court said, "Attorney Harris, you may show the witness your photographs."

To say Albury was now prepared for the worst was an understatement. He looked, panic-stricken, in Dan's direction, but received no succor.

I went through each shot with him, eliciting his reluctant agreement that they showed him stuffing both sticks in the same evidence bag. His once confident mien had been reduced to a frantic whisper. At the end, I asked, "You defined contamination as occurring when certain evidence comes too close to other evidence, and what was on the one gets on the other, right?"

He didn't answer and looked down at some unseen object on the floor.

"Right, Detective?"

"Yes."

"And therefore, isn't it true that contamination may have occurred here, when you placed both objects in the bag together?"

Albury shot one last needy look at Dan, and said, "Yes."

I looked at the jury. They were certainly a little confused because they had only heard that Bob's DNA had been found on one of the sticks in Dan's opening statement, but they also knew something important had just happened and looked concerned over the patent disregard of standard procedures in the collection of this evidence.

Chapter Thirty-Four

I had done my homework on the snitch, Stephen Baxter. I had subpoenaed his criminal and prison records. His rap sheet went back fifteen years, mostly petty B & E's but also a few check kiting and larceny charges. I liked those last ones—they showed a flair for deceptiveness. One of the larcenies involved a theft from Baxter's then employer. I was not surprised to see Jerry Lathrop had been the arresting officer on two of the house break-ins. I had suspected as much, and now was certain who was behind Baxter's testimony.

Dan called him as his next witness. I knew he was in his late twenties, and by my reckoning, had spent a third of his young life in prison. He looked like it—a ghost-like pall enveloped him, due certainly to the few hours each day he spent outside. He also had a smart-aleck composure and rarely looked Dan or me in the eye when testifying.

Dan set the stage by having him relate in detail the dates he was held in the same protective custody wing of the jail with Bob. The exact timing of his contact and conversation had not been revealed in the initial police report. I armed Ben with the prison records to follow along with Baxter's statements. At the end of Thompson's direct examination,

Ben pointed to a section of the records which he had highlighted.

I decided to start my cross-examination with impeaching Baxter's credibility with his criminal history. There's a certain way you need to do this. You start by asking the witness, "Are you the same Stephen Baxter who, on May 30, 2011 was convicted of breaking and entering a dwelling house?" If the witness doesn't remember, or denies it, you show him the record to refresh his recollection and admit the record into evidence.

Here, Baxter readily admitted his nefarious past. He almost seemed to be proud of it. After I had reached his seventh conviction on the B & E's and walked him through the larcenies, I could sense the jury had little belief in his capacity for truth-telling.

I pulled out the police reports I had summonsed relating to two of his break-in's. "Mr. Baxter, you know that Mr. Wilson is now standing trial for the murder of Frances Lathrop, don't you?"

"Of course. The one he admitted killing."

"And you know Frances' father is Jerry Lathrop?"

"Yeah."

"You've spoken to him before, right?"

"If you want to call it that. He's arrested me a couple of times."

"Didn't Officer Lathrop, or someone from the Key West Police Department, talk to you about testifying against Mr. Wilson?"

Dan objected, citing the lack of a foundation for my line of inquiry. The judge allowed me to continue, admonishing me to get specific about the basis for my questions.

"Absolutely not."

"Isn't it true, Mr. Baxter, that the prosecutor and the police promised you some consideration, like an early release on parole, for coming in here and lying about a conversation you had with this defendant?"

This time Dan's vehement objection was sustained, and Judge Thorpe ordered me to pursue another avenue of questioning. I didn't care. I had placed the suggestion of impropriety between the prosecution and this witness squarely in the jurors' minds.

It was time for the coup de grâce. "Mr. Baxter, I believe you testified on direct examination that you were placed in the protective custody section of the jail from July 25 through August 10, is that right?"

"Approximately. I'm not positive about the exact dates."

"But somewhere in there, right?"

"Right."

"And I heard you pinpoint the date of your conversation with Mr. Wilson as August 10, correct?"

"Well, I had many conversations with him. But it was on August 10 that he admitted he killed that poor girl."

Good old Mr. Baxter was playing this to the hilt. He choked up briefly while making this last statement.

"You're sure of that date because the very next day, August 11, you were paroled from the jail, correct."

"Yeah."

"You wouldn't forget that date, right? It was important to you?"

"Nope. I was getting out."

"Right. Your release date. No one forgets that."

He looked at me blankly. I could see a recognition in his eyes that I was up to something. "If you say so."

"I don't say so, Mr. Baxter. You said it. Just a minute ago."

"I guess so."

His otherwise cocky exterior had quickly morphed into a dark surliness.

"Now, Mr. Baxter, I have some records here that purport to be certified records of your imprisonment at the Monroe County Correctional Center from May 30 to August 11. Have you ever seen these before?" I handed him a copy of the records.

He took them and looked confused. I had given a copy of the same records to Dan just prior to commencing my examination. Dan started to rise in protest, then apparently realized he had no grounds for an objection.

"Mr. Baxter," I continued, "Do you see the highlighted portion of those documents that says, "Term of Incarceration?"

He paused, found the section I was referring to, and said, "Yeah."

"And that says you were in the jail from May 30 to August 11, right?"

"Yeah. That's right. I got out on August 11, the day after Bobby confessed to me."

"That's what you've said. I'm going to ask you to turn the page and look at the boxes I've also highlighted for you."

He did so and looked, obviously not comprehending what he was looking at.

"Does that box on the left say, "July 25 – inmate admitted to Protective custody?"

"It does, and I think I testified that was the date I was transferred there."

"Yes, you did. Now let's look at the box on the right. Doesn't that say, 'Date of Transfer out of Protective Custody?'"

"Ah…yep." Then his face, including his ears, reddened. "Wait. This is all wrong. This says I was moved out of PC on August 9. That's not right." He was shouting now.

"But that's exactly what the official record shows, doesn't it, Mr. Baxter? That you were moved out of PC the day before you've testified Mr. Wilson made those statements to you."

"I'm telling you, that's an error. I know when I left."

"Okay, so you're right, and these certified State records are wrong. Were any of the records of your past crimes wrong, Mr. Baxter?"

He didn't answer. For the first time, he held my gaze, this time with the most malicious eyes I had ever encountered.

"When you stole money from your employer, did you lie to him about taking it?"

"Objection, Your Honor," Dan screamed.

"Sustained," Judge Thorpe ruled.

I successfully offered the prison records into evidence, and said,

"That's all I have of this witness," giving Baxter a scornful look.

Chapter Thirty-Five

The prosecution called Dr. Carlos Attila as its DNA expert. I knew he was affiliated with the Mayo Clinic in Minnesota and world-renowned in DNA research. It didn't matter to me, because I wasn't going to contest any of his findings.

I did have my work cut out for me, however, on the contamination issue. I knew he would be forewarned and primed to respond to any questions on that subject. So, I contacted Dr. Gordon and asked him to come to Key West during Attila's testimony to advise me on my best line of questioning.

Gordon came down the night before so we could catch dinner and drinks at Prime, one of the best steakhouses in town. Henry had previously mentioned he liked the beef.

The only semblance of Key West at Prime is the attire of the patrons. It doesn't matter what you dress like down here so long as you're wearing a shirt, pants and sandals, and even these requirements are often waived. In New York, Chicago, or any other sophisticated urban center, customers of a high-class surf and turf restaurant would most likely be garbed in a suit or jacket and tie, or evening dresses. Tonight, flip-flops, shorts and tank tops were the dominate dress code.

During dinner, I found out Henry was married with three boys, ranging in age from twelve to seventeen. Although having no children of my own, I was impressed with parents who spent most of their free time with their kids. Henry obviously adored his sons and had taken them everywhere—hiking in many of the National Parks, camping throughout Europe, and even mountain climbing in the Rockies. I didn't have children because I innately knew I was too selfish. If you are going to have them, you should damn well be ready to sacrifice for them.

He brought some reading materials for me on DNA contamination. Nothing too scientific—more geared toward making the subject comprehensible to the average citizen. He told me not to back off on the issue with Attila, who he also realized would be locked and loaded to respond to my questioning.

Dr. Attila took the stand at ten the next morning. He was as impressive looking as I had imagined—light grey flannel suit, dark blue shirt, cream-colored paisley tie. A bit on the short side—maybe 5'9", but great posture that made him look taller than his actual stature.

Dan ran him through the facts we already knew—Frances' and an unknown male's DNA was on one stick, Bob's on both. It didn't surprise me when Dan opened the subject of contamination. It's always best to try to defuse an issue as soon as possible in a trial. Dan had Attila define the word, and then got down to business: "Dr. Attila, are you aware the defense in this case has raised the issue of contamination of evidence?"

I decided to object, only to be able to make a short speech in front of the jury. "Your Honor, we didn't raise the issue of contamination. The prosecution did by combining two pieces of evidence in one bag. That's . . ."

"Enough, Attorney Harris," the judge interrupted. "Overruled."

I sat down, feigning a look of disappointment.

"You may answer the question," Dan said to the witness.

"Yes, I am aware of that."

"Even if the two sticks of wood were placed in the same evidence bag, as alleged by the defense in this case, would that cause contamination of evidence?"

"Probably not," Attila answered.

I looked at the jury with bewilderment, as if I couldn't believe what Attila was saying.

"Why not?"

"Because the two sticks were only in the evidence bag a short time, and as I understand it, the evidence bag in question was divided into two separate compartments."

Now where in the hell did that come from?

Dan approached closer to the jury. "So, Doctor, because that evidence was only in the bag a short time, and the items were kept apart, there was no contamination?"

"As I said, most probably not."

Dan looked at the jury with a victorious I-told-you-so expression, and at me with disdain. "Your witness, counsel."

I leaned over to Ben "That was a zinger."

"Hold on Sam," Ben replied. "Ask the judge for a brief recess."

I didn't question his request, and the judge adjourned for a half-hour morning break.

"What do you have in mind?" I asked Ben.

Ben sauntered nonchalantly over to the prosecution table. I overheard him say, "Dan, can I see exhibits eighteen and nineteen? You know, the murder weapon and other stick?" Even though they had already been introduced into evidence, Dan still had them on his desk, in different, sealed plastic bags.

"Well, sure, but be careful."

"Oh, I will." Ben looked at the items intently, then suddenly bent down and reached under the table. He quickly extracted a bag that perfectly resembled the evidence bags in the photographs. "Oh, what's this, Dan?"

Dan's eyes stretched wide. "Hey, put that back."

"Isn't this a typical evidence bag?"

"Well, one kind, not the kind that carried the sticks from

the murder scene."

"Oh, Okay," Ben said. "Why don't we leave this here right on the edge of the desk," and without waiting for an answer, Ben placed it on the desk closest to the jury. I saw quickly there were no separate compartments in the bag. Dan protested, but went silent when Ben threatened to take the issue before the judge. Ben walked back to our defense table and gave me an exaggerated wink.

I had my cue. When Attila resumed the stand, my first question was, after I presented Ralph's photos of the evidence gathering to him, "Doctor, you've seen these photos before, haven't you?"

"Yes, I believe they're the ones Mr. Thompson showed me."

"You know they show the two sticks being placed in the same evidence bag, right?"

"Yes, I suppose so."

I approached the witness with the photographs in hand. "Doctor, can you see any compartments, any separation in the bag in the photographs?"

"No, but I was told they were in there."

"Told by Mr. Thompson?"

"Yes, I believe so."

I picked up the bag Ben had placed on Dan's desk. "Doctor, doesn't this look identical to the bag in the pictures?"

"Objection," Dan screamed. "That bag is not in evidence."

"No, he may have it, subject to a motion to strike," Thorpe replied.

"Well, kinda," the witness responded.

"Kinda, Doctor? Isn't it the same color, same shape, same dimensions?"

"It appears to be, but I can't say for sure."

"You were never shown an evidence bag that had a separation inside, were you?"

"Well . . . no . . . just told."

"That's right, just told. But here's an identical bag, right in front of you, and please show me where it's compartmentalized so different items of evidence can be kept apart." I handed him the bag.

"Clearly this is not the same bag, because there aren't separate compartments."

I turned toward the judge, still keeping the jury in my line of sight. "Judge, I hereby demand that the prosecution produce such a bag as they claim the evidence was placed into, one with separate compartments. Until I see such a bag, I am offering this one as Defendant's Exhibit One.

"Objection, Your Honor." Dan's timbre was edged with panic.

"Overruled. Defendant's Exhibit One is admitted."

I felt that Judge Thorpe was beginning to lean toward our side.

"Now Doctor," I resumed. "If this Exhibit was, or was identical to, the actual bag that housed the murder weapon and the other piece of wood, wouldn't you admit the possibility of contamination would be greatly increased?"

Attila was befuddled. His once superior mien had cracked like an eggshell. I noticed his legs going up and down rapidly from their bent position in the witness box.

"Dr. Attila, please answer the question."

He still hesitated, his eyes darting around a spot on the carpet in front of him. Finally, he whispered, "Yes."

"What was that?" I demanded. "We couldn't hear you."

"Yes," in a barely more audible tone.

I had accomplished my purpose. You don't keep an opposing expert witness on the stand any longer than necessary to drive home your point. I said, with a disgusted look, "I have no further questions of this witness," and returned to our table.

Chapter Thirty-Six

Dan called his next and, as he dramatically announced to the packed courtroom, his last witness: Mrs. Betty Lathrop. My mouth hung open as a short, mousey woman, with stringy black hair and thin to the point of emaciation, walked up the aisle. Even though she was on Dan's list, she was the last person I thought he would use as a witness. What about Jerry? What was she going to offer that he could not? I smelled a big, stinky rat.

As Dan got into his questioning, a realization slowly dawned on me. She was the one, not Jerry, who was going to introduce their daughter to the jury, to humanize her, gain sympathy for her, be the voice of the dead. I turned toward Ben and said, "What's going on here?"

He looked pensive but quickly replied, "I don't think they're going to use Jerry, and I think we know why."

Damn. If he was right I'd have to call him as my witness, which made things more difficult. Then I could only directly, as opposed to cross, examine him. A lawyer could control a witness and the scope of his testimony much better with cross-examination.

I also realized I had never seen Betty Lathrop before, even

during the long hours I had staked out their home. Her pale complexion told me she rarely went outside.

Dan had her describe her daughter, what she looked like, the activities she enjoyed. She lugubriously related in gut-wrenching detail how she found out about Frances' death, and her traumatic reaction to it. She broke down several times and sobbed, Dan gratuitously providing her with Kleenex each time. Frances did sound like a very sweet child. When Dan had finished, there was not a dry eye in the jury.

It was my turn. I had to be careful, not wanting to look like the bad guy. Just before I stood up to question her, Ben whispered in my ear, "Did you notice how she referred to her husband throughout as 'Mr. Lathrop?'"

I thought for a second and said, "Wow, you're right."

I immediately expressed my sympathy to Mrs. Lathrop over the death of her daughter. Then I got to the point.

"Mrs. Lathrop, do you recall having a conversation with Lieutenant Milbury on July 14?"

She paused. Did I detect a slight "tell" in her left eye—a momentary tic in her eyelid?

"Um...no...um, I'm not sure."

I pulled out the redacted police report and said, "Let the record show I am presenting the witness with a report dated July 15, from Lieutenant Milbury with the Monroe County Sheriff's Office, a report provided to me by the prosecution."

Dan moved as if to stand, then looked like he thought better of it. I knew he'd surely be objecting in a few seconds.

"Mrs. Lathrop, I'm going to draw your attention to the paragraph in this report starting with the words, *I was finally able to meet with Betty Lathrop at her home on Twelfth Street*, and ending just before the blacked-out portion. Please read it to yourself."

She read it with a quizzical look. Then I noticed a strange gleam form in her eyes. At first I thought she was going to lash out at me, but she remained silent.

"Doesn't that say that Lieutenant Milbury spoke to you on July 14?"

"Yes, it does," she said calmly.

I got the distinct impression she *wanted* to repeat her statement.

"Didn't you tell the Lieutenant that…"

Dan had sprung to his feet and loudly interrupted me. "I strongly object, Your Honor. That portion of the report was redacted because it contains a privileged communication between this witness and her husband."

The judge motioned us over to the side of his bench. "What's this all about, Attorney Harris?" he asked.

"Judge, even though the prosecution attempted to redact the conversation, I was very easily able to read the words through a bright light," I explained. "It contains a statement from Mrs. Lathrop that is highly incriminating of Mr. Lathrop."

"Are you suggesting that Officer Lathrop had something to do with the death of his daughter?" the judge asked.

It was time to let the cat out of the bag. "That's exactly what I'm suggesting, Judge. And there will be additional, credible evidence to support that hypothesis."

"That's outrageous, Your Honor," Dan said. "Attorney Harris is trying to lead us down a rabbit hole that has no end."

"But I can't prevent him from introducing evidence that someone else perpetrated the crime, even if that person is a cop and the girl's father," Judge Thorpe said. "And isn't this a statement Mrs. Lathrop gave voluntarily to the police?"

"Well, yes, judge. But it was a private communication between a husband and a wife."

"But, Attorney Thompson, that privilege was waived as soon as she repeated the conversation to the police."

"That's correct, Your Honor," I said.

"I respectfully disagree, Judge," Dan said, "but there's also the spousal exclusion. As you know, a spouse cannot testify against the other in a criminal proceeding without the consent of the other spouse, and I can represent to the court that Jerry Lathrop adamantly objects to his wife repeating this conversation."

"I'm not so sure that applies here where Mr. Lathrop isn't the defendant, but I do want to hear from him personally if he wants to assert the testimonial privilege. Bailiff, let's give the jury a recess. Mr. Thompson, is Mr. Lathrop outside?"

"Yes, he is, Judge."

The jury was escorted out, and a court officer went out to get

Jerry Lathrop. He came in, a confused look on his face.

"Mr. Lathrop," the Judge said, "you have a right to object to your wife testifying in court concerning matters that might expose you to criminal liability. I've been informed she made a statement to the police that might just do that."

Jerry's mien quickly morphed from confusion to rage. "What?" he shouted, looking at Betty. "What did you say to them?"

"Mr. Lathrop, please control yourself," the judge warned. "Do you or do you not want to assert the privilege?"

There was no consoling Jerry Lathrop. "I have no idea what this is all about, and I certainly don't want my wife testifying, but . . ." and he turned toward Betty," but you fuckin' bitch, what have you done?"

Betty Lathrop cowered in the witness chair.

"Mr. Lathrop, this is your final warning," Judge Thorpe bellowed. "Okay, I'm not going to allow the statement in. I think Mr. Lathrop has a right to prevent his spouse from testifying."

I was about to speak when I saw Betty Lathrop timidly raise her hand and motion to the judge. I had no idea what she wanted, but all my legal instincts told me to let her have her say.

"Judge Thorpe," I said. "I think the witness wants to say something to us."

The Judge turned toward Betty. "What is it, Mrs. Lathrop?"

I could barely hear the words, but there was no mistaking them.

"Jerry and I are not *really* married."

All hell broke loose. Jerry ran toward the witness stand, his arms extended as if to seize her by the throat. He was tackled by a court officer just inches from reaching her.

Once he was handcuffed, the Judge ordered him to be brought before him. "Mr. Lathrop, I should find you in contempt of court, both for that outburst, but also for representing to this court that you're married to this witness."

"But, Your Honor," he pleaded. "We *are* married. We're common law spouses."

Judge Thorpe said, "Mr. Lathrop. There are no common-law marriages in Florida. Do you have a valid marriage certificate?"

"Ah . . . no. I thought as long as we lived together for seven years, we were common law spouses."

"No, you're not, and the statement can come in."

The Judge ordered a court officer to accompany Jerry Lathrop out of the courtroom, and asked the officer to stay with him the duration of Betty Lathrop's testimony. The jury was brought back in, and I resumed my examination. Betty added some additional juicy details to her statement to Lieutenant Milbury. She testified that Jerry also said that "he was going to teach that girl once and for all," and the day after the murder she saw that the shoes he wore the prior night were still sandy and wet.

Dan didn't ask any questions, a tactic I knew was designed so that Betty's testimony would not be indelibly ingrained in the jury's minds through needless repetition. There was a barely perceptible, but unmistakable, change in the atmosphere in the courtroom. I could see it in the jurors' eyes. They sensed there was another alternative to the prosecution's theory that Bob had committed the crime.

Chapter Thirty-Seven

Dan rested and the judge granted me a welcome recess until the next morning to present my case. I met with Ben that evening, over coffee, not whiskey, at the Starbucks on the ground floor of the La Concha Hotel on Duval Street. The first order of business was my opening statement. I had already given a great amount of thought to it.

One option in any opening is to lay out in detail what you expect to prove. The problem with that is, I have found, juries are not happy when you fail to live up to your promises. This case was far too fraught with uncertainties to do that. We still didn't know whether Bob was going to testify; Jerry Lathrop was a complete unknown; and I wasn't sure the judge would allow Janine's testimony on the DNA evidence or even Dr. Gordon's findings. Sally's testimony had parts that were objectionable. Ben and I agreed, I would make a very general opening reminding the jury there was another, very viable option for the perpetrator of this crime.

When we showed up the next morning for trial, Ben and I placed an empty chair between us at the defense counsel table. On it we placed a foam board, containing an outline of a human male figure with a large question mark where the face should have been. I was more than surprised when Dan didn't object to my shenanigans, and Judge Thorpe, God bless him, said nothing.

I dressed a little more formally and conservatively for this day. This was the time to impress upon the jury the seriousness of their duty. I donned a black suit I only wore for funerals, and white button-down shirt and brown tie. I tried to remind myself, throughout the day, to stop yanking at the starched collar that felt like a garrote.

As I was getting up to present my opening, Ben tapped me on the shoulder and motioned to the gallery behind us with his thumb. I looked back, and saw Betty Lathrop seated directly behind us. The symbolism, I was sure, was not lost on the jury. She had joined our side.

I introduced myself, Ben, and Bob again, personalizing Bob with his first name only. You never refer to your client as "Mr." or as "the defendant." Your client is just one of the plain folk.

I also ran through the rights that are afforded a person accused of a crime, starting with the presumption of innocence and ending with the right not to testify. As to that latter, which is the most important if you're not going to call your guy to testify, or you're unsure whether you are or not, I go further than the canned instruction the court usually gives: that the Fifth Amendment to the United States Constitution guarantees someone accused of a crime the right not to be forced to testify on his own behalf.

I always say the following: "There are many reasons an absolutely innocent person may decide not to testify. It could be that the prosecution has such a weak case there's no need to explain anything. Or it could be that the accused is poor at public speaking. But the major point is that the jury, as a fundamental constitutional right of a defendant, may not speculate on the reasons."

Then I said: "Now you have heard some evidence that someone else other than Bob committed this crime. And you know who I'm talking about." I walked over to the chair with the foam board figure perched on it. "This is the man who should be sitting here at the defendant's table, not Bob." I placed my arm around Bob's shoulder. "This is an innocent man, ladies and gentlemen of the jury, and when you've heard our side of this case, you'll know what you have to do—come back with a not guilty verdict. The defense calls Janine Reynolds."

Ben and I had much earlier decided to go first with the DNA evidence, which surely was the most damaging to the prosecution's case. I had arranged with Janine and her mother to hide out in the ladies room until they received our text message, which Ben sent just as I was beginning my opening. When no one came through the door as I announced my first witness, I motioned for Ben to go out to the hallway to retrieve her.

I said to the judge, "Your Honor, she should be right outside."

Ben spent a good half-minute outside, then reentered with a shrug and a strange expression on his face. I motioned him up to our table. He whispered in my ear, "I have no clue where they are. I'm sure they understood our instructions."

I approached the bench and Dan came up. I told Judge Thorpe my dilemma, and he granted me a five-minute recess to find her.

Ben and I scoured the entire courthouse. I even enlisted several court officers I knew well, one a female who searched the ladies room. I also called and texted Janine several times. Ben stayed outside the courtroom to wait until she came back.

Judge Thorpe asked if I was ready with another witness. I had asked Ralph DiPiero to come in as a back-up, which is always a good thing to do in any trial. I wasn't worried about Janine . . . yet . . . I knew her to be daffy enough to have lost track of time.

Ralph was great. I had blown up the relevant photos and mounted them on 3′ x 5′ foam boards. He described where he took the shots and the active steps behind the scenes of the still photos. I thought by the time he finished there was little doubt the two sticks had been placed, touching one another, in the same evidence bag. Dan did little to challenge that point.

When I had finished with Ralph, Ben, who had been waiting for Janine and monitoring the progress of the trial, came fully into the court room. He looked exasperated, and worried. Now *I* was worried.

I apprised the judge of my concerns, and he asked Dan to call Albury and Phillips up to the dais. He addressed us together. "Gentlemen, Attorney Harris advises me he had a witness, Janine Reynolds, in the courthouse ready to testify. She was with her mother. They were in the ladies room awaiting a call to come into the court room. Now they can't be found. I'm asking for the prosecution's assistance on this. This is a matter of the proper administration of justice. Let's find Janine Reynolds."

"We'll do the best we can," Dan said.

I didn't believe a word of it. "Judge," I cut in as Dan and his entourage turned to leave. "Can we also include Lieutenant Millbury in the hunt? He's been actively involved in the case from the get-go." Millbury was the one guy I trusted. He was the one who took the initiative to visit Betty when her husband was away.

"That sounds like a good idea," Judge Thorpe said. He was so far into our camp it would have taken a bolt from heaven to turn him against us.

Ben had called Cody and Tyler during the break and they came right over. I knew they thought it was cool they were going to testify at a murder trial. They focused well during my interviews with them so I felt confident they were ready.

Both did, in fact, do a great job. Cody explained our chance meeting in the jail cell, and the mechanics he used to pull the photographs from the iCloud. Tyler related how he had enlarged and clarified the photos, which I had also mounted on large foam boards Dan raised numerous objections to their testimony and the admission of the selfies, but Thorpe thwarted him at every turn. I felt Dan's frequent objections led the jury to believe he was trying to cover up the truth. My 3' x 5' blowups of those photos were admitted, which, with the judge's permission, I placed on easels next to our table for the jury to see every time they looked our way.

I couldn't ask the witnesses what the photographs depicted, as that would transgress on the jury's duty of evaluating the evidence. But I could tell by the look in the jurors' eyes they realized if in fact it was Francis and her killer in the background, then certainly Bob, who was standing in the foreground with Harley, could not have killed the girl.

Chapter Thirty-Eight

By the time I had finished with Ralph, Cody and Tyler, it was almost three o'clock in the afternoon. I had Ben call Sally to come in but I hated to present my case in such a disorganized, haphazard way. Yes, our primary job as defense counsel is to confuse and disrupt the prosecution's presentation, but if we put on a case, it must follow an orderly, comprehensible path to the inescapable conclusion of—not guilty.

I approached the bench and motioned Ben over. Judge Thorpe asked Dan what the progress was in finding Janine and her mom. Dan called a uniformed officer, who had just recently come into the court room, up to the dais. He said, "Judge, this is Officer Leary. I haven't heard anything, but maybe he has."

Leary had just gotten through the swinging gate into our area when his radio crackled loudly, and a voice yelled, "Shots fired. Officer down. Officer down." We, as well as the jury, flinched noticeably. Leary quickly replaced the earpiece that had been dangling over his shoulder into his ear and spoke quietly into the mike attached to the lapel of his shirt. He listened, then tried to pull Dan aside.

"No officer, I want to hear this," Thorpe said. "Bailiff, excuse the jury." Thorpe put up his hand in a gesture that said to us, stay put and no further conversation in front of the jury.

Once the last juror had exited the room, the judge said, "Okay, what's going on here?"

I could tell by Leary's posture he desperately wanted to get out of there and respond to the call.

"Well, your honor," Leary said. "It looks like they found the missing witness. Is her last name Williams?"

I realized they had found Janine, but I feared the worst. I said, "That's also a name she uses, judge."

Judge Thorpe excused the officer with an admonition to have someone report to him right away.

They took Bob back to the lock-up and Ben and I sat in the lobby waiting to hear any news. I kept trying Janine, but she failed to pick up.

In what seemed like a millennium, but was only an hour, I saw Dan, with Albury and Milbury in tow, stride quickly into the courtroom. Ben and I followed. The session clerk led us into the judge's chambers. We were seated in a semi-circle around the judge's immense desk.

"All right. Give me the short version," Thorpe said.

Dan responded. "Things are extremely confused now, judge. But it seems that a Key West police officer forced Janine Williams, also known as Janine Reynolds, and her mother Alice Williams, out of the courthouse bathroom at gunpoint, and drove them to an abandoned house over on William Street near the Casa Marina."

"What was the name of the officer?" I asked.

Dan glared at me, then said, "It was Officer Stearn."

I gave a knowing look to Ben.

"Do we know where they are now?" Thorpe inquired.

Dan replied, "Yes, at the station. It looks like Alice Williams was armed, and shot officer Stearn. He is deceased. We're holding them for questioning."

"Judge, I need to go over there right now," I said. "I will be representing both ladies from this point on. Can we recess until tomorrow morning?"

"Of course," Thorpe said.

Ben and I hopped into a cab and handed the cabbie a twenty with instructions to hoof it to the police station pronto. We arrived in less than five minutes.

We were escorted into the detectives' room. I saw Janine and Alice sitting across from Phillips. They did not appear to be injured, even though Alice had obviously been crying and looked disheveled. Janine gave me a fierce, determined look.

"What's going on here?" I asked, as I approached them.

"Have a seat, Sam," Phillips said.

I was sure that was the first time I'd ever heard him call me "Sam." I sat down in the seat offered by the direction of his hand. Ben stood off to the side.

"Here's what we know," Phillips began. "Janine and Alice were in the ladies room when Stearn barged in with gun drawn. He ordered them to come with him. He led them in handcuffs out to his patrol car."

"With his jacket draped over the gun so no one could see it," Alice piped in. Janine nodded her head affirmatively.

"He took them to a vacant structure in the Casa Marina area."

"He had a key to the back door," Janine added.

"Inside," Phillips continued, "Stearn threatened to shoot them if they tried to escape. He had two old mattresses on the floor."

"That smelled like rat piss," Alice said.

"He also told them exactly what had happened to Frances Lathrop. It's almost unbelievable."

"I always thought he was a pervert," Janine said.

"Stearn told the ladies he and Lathrop had a homosexual relationship. The afternoon of the murder, Frances came home unexpectedly early from school. Betty Lathrop was at a friend's house. Frances opened the door to the bedroom where Stearn and Lathrop were having sex. Lathrop strangled her to death on the spot. They then both raped and sodomized her. They loaded her into Stearn's police cruiser and dropped her body by the Salt Ponds. They planted her bike at the scene to make it look like she had ridden over there on her own. They then bludgeoned her with a piece of wood they found at the location to make it look like the killing took place there."

"We couldn't believe he was telling us all that, but it sure convinced us he was not going to let us live," Alice said.

Phillips said, "Stearn left the structure. While he was away, the two ladies oriented themselves so Janine was able to pull her mother's pistol out of a thigh holster she had under her skirt. When Stearn came back, she ordered Stearn to unlock the handcuffs. He pulled his service revolver, and Janine shot him twice through the heart."

I looked at Janine incredulously.

"My mommy taught me well," she said.

I thought I detected a smirk on Alice's lips.

"Are there any charges being filed here?" I asked.

"Not at all," Phillips said. "We've confirmed everything they've told us. All we need to do is compare Stearn's DNA to that found on the murder weapon. I have no doubt it will match."

"So, we're free to go?" I asked.

"Absolutely."

The four of us, the girls, Ben and I, made our way quickly to Louie's. We all needed a drink. Bad. Very bad.

I got the full, first-hand version of what happened from Janine and Alice. They were convinced Stearn wasn't just going to keep them on ice for the duration of the trial. He needed to destroy the evidence of his crimes, which meant burying Janine and Alice's bodies in a place even the land crabs couldn't find. The thought gave me the shudders.

"I really don't think you're in a condition to testify tomorrow," I told Janine, "after what you've been through."

"I'm ready," she said. "I'm sure that asshole Lathrop was behind the whole thing."

I had to agree with her.

"Honey, your direct is one thing. Dan Thompson is going to try to hammer you into a bent nail if he can on cross. I don't want to put you through that right away."

"I can deal with it."

Ben cut in. "I've got an idea. I think Lathrop's at the end of his rope. Why don't we try to put an end to this horrible affair once and for all. Call Jerry Lathrop to the stand first thing tomorrow morning. We'll be unrelenting. We've always got Janine, Dr. Gordon, and even Sally as back-up if we need. Let's see if we can't break the jerk."

I looked around the table. Everyone nodded their heads in agreement. "Okay. First thing tomorrow. Let's go for Jerry Lathrop's jugular."

Chapter Thirty-Nine

I called the constable I regularly use, to serve a new subpoena on Lathrop to appear in the morning at courtroom D. He was already under a general subpoena issued by the court to show up every day trial was conducted, but I didn't want him to have any wiggle room. There could be no excuse with the new subpoena. Also, I wanted him to stew about what I might be up to.

Ben and I went back to my house to prepare the examination of Lathrop. We set out the general parameters: who he really was; did he have prior children and a wife; did he see them? Did he know Sally Berkshire or Janine Reynolds; did he have the conversation with his wife… well… girlfriend, that she had repeated; where was he at the time of Frances' murder? We expected he'd deny taking on his brother's identification, but our primary mission tomorrow was to rattle the crap out of him.

Ben and I arrived at the courthouse at nine sharp the next morning. As usual, we showed our Florida State Bar cards to the court officer manning the metal detector, and walked around it. A small perk still allowed attorneys. I noticed Jerry Lathrop up ahead, today in his full-dress uniform, enter the same way with some other police officers. To my surprise, I looked back and saw Betty Lathrop enter the same way. I guessed she was afforded that courtesy as the wife of a cop.

Jerry was already sitting on the bench closest to the courtroom doors when we arrived upstairs. He got up as we approached. Ben and I stopped in our tracks, and I crouched slightly, ready to thwart an attack. He stopped ten feet in front of us. There were, as usual, two court officers in the vicinity. I could see them eye us warily.

Lathrop pulled the subpoena out of his back pocket, shook it in front of us, and yelled, "What is this shit, Harris? What are you trying to do?"

"Why, Mr. Lathrop, that's a subpoena," I said with exaggerated calmness. "You've seen them before."

"Look Harris. Your fucked-up client killed my daughter, and now you serve me with process. I ought to tear your head off right now."

Both court officers had narrowed the gap between us during our first colloquy, and now they came running over the rest of the way.

"Gentlemen" I said to them. "There's no problem here. I'm sure Mr. Lathrop is going to let us enter the courtroom without incident, aren't you Mr. Lathrop?"

He glowered at me, then stepped to the side.

We entered the courtroom and took our seats. Dan and his entourage were already there. There were no cordialities exchanged. I was sure he knew about Jerry's subpoena. Bob was brought in. I explained briefly what had happened to Janine and Alice. He looked incredulous. I noticed Betty Lathrop take her seat two rows behind us.

Judge Thorpe came to the bench and asked me if I was ready with a witness. I told him we were, and he ordered the jury brought in.

When they were seated, Thorpe nodded at me. I stood and said, "The defense calls Jerry Lathrop." A collective sound of surprise wafted around the courtroom, enough so that Judge Thorpe pounded his gavel and said in a stern voice, "Silence. Bailiff, I assume Mr. Lathrop is outside. Bring him in, please."

I looked back and saw Lathrop come in with a court officer, the one who had just witnessed our brief encounter, close by his side. Lathrop had a hideous expression on his face—contorted, a harsh mixture of rage and hate. Thorpe asked him to take the witness stand.

He had to pass directly in front of the jury to get to the stand. I saw each of them instinctively recoil, his anger was so palpable. I noticed his hand shake uncontrollably as he raised it to take the oath.

His eyes turned black as he looked toward me.

I asked him to state his full name, which he agreed was Jerald A. Lathrop, and address for the record, and had him relate that he was a Key West Police Officer, out on disability for a year. He also stated he was the father of the late Frances Lathrop. I quickly got him to agree his father was Edgar Lathrop, and his mother Marian, née Cartwright.

Then I stepped closer to him, no more than three feet from the witness stand. I could almost feel at this distance the repel of the opposing forces between us, as if the positive and negative terminals of a powerful magnet were being thrust together.

"You had a brother who passed away about fifteen years ago, didn't you Mr. Lathrop?"

Lathrop half stood out of the witness chair. "What does that have to do with your client raping and killing my daughter?" he screamed.

Judge Thorpe slammed his gavel, and motioned a court officer over.

"Mr. Lathrop," Thorpe commanded. "Get control of yourself."

Dan had stood and now objected to my question. Thorpe called us to the side bar, and said once we got there, "First, Mr. Thompson, someone needs to talk to this witness about getting himself under control. Is the Chief here?" He looked around.

"No, Judge but I can call him if you like."

"Well, let's see if I can handle it. Mr. Lathrop," the judge continued, "Mr. Thompson is the one to object to Mr. Harris' questions. And I am the one who keeps order in this court. Do you understand that, sir?"

Lathrop nodded. I could still feel he was a grenade with the pin half-pulled.

"I'm going to allow Mr. Harris a little latitude, here," Thorpe said, "but let's get quickly to your point for calling him, Mr. Harris."

I nodded, and returned to the same spot in front of the witness.

"Did you understand my question, Mr. Lathrop?"

He still hesitated, then murmured, "Michael."

"Did you say Michael, Mr. Lathrop?"

"Yeah."

"Your brother was older than you, wasn't he?"

"Yeah, I guess so."

I raised my voice a notch. "You *guess so*, Mr. Lathrop. Was he older than you or not?"

Lathrop shifted in his seat. "Yeah, older."

"Was he born on October 8, 1981?"

Lathrop was licking his lips furiously. "I'm not good with dates."

"Okay. But didn't he pass away on June 15, 2001?"

"Again, I'm bad on dates."

"Were his birth and death at least close to those dates, Mr. Lathrop?" I feigned a tone of exasperation.

"I guess."

I turned and walked back to counsel table. Ben had already retrieved a folder and laid it on the front of our table closest to me. I picked it up, extracted two sheets of paper from it, and walked back to the witness. Ben quickly got up and placed copies of the papers on Dan's table.

I said, "I have here what purport to be certified copies of the birth and death certificates of an individual with the last name of Lathrop…who appears to have been born, and died on those very same dates, and whose father was Edgar Lathrop, and mother Mary Cartwright Lathrop."

I could tell by Jerry's staccato shaking of his leg up and down that he now realized where I was going. Dan, I'm sure, saw it too, and realized he better object, which he did. Thorpe again said he'd give me a few more questions on the subject. I could tell I had him interested.

I handed the documents to Jerry. "Doesn't that first one say that Jerald A. Lathrop was born on October 8, 1981?"

He stared blankly at the document.

"Doesn't that second one say that individual died on June 15, 2001?"

Again, no answer.

"Mr. Lathop, is it not true that your brother's name was Jerald A. Lathrop, and that he was born and died on the aforementioned dates?"

Dan jumped to his feet and screamed his objection. Thorpe sustained his objection, and told me to move on to another subject. But I wasn't quite finished.

"And Mr. Lathrop, isn't it true you assumed your brother's identity after his death, and that your true name is Michael Lathrop?"

Judge Thorpe's gavel struck hard. "Attorney Harris, I told you to move on to another subject. So do it."

I managed to look somewhat repentant, but I snuck a peek at the jury. They were mesmerized.

"Now Mr. Lathrop, you've always held yourself out to be married to Betty Lathrop, haven't you?"

"As far as I'm concerned, I'm married to her."

"But you know now there are no common-law marriages in

Florida, so without a marriage certificate and recognized ceremony, you're not married in the eyes of the State of Florida, right?"

"Well, I am in the eyes of God."

"Answer the question, Mr. Lathrop. But not according to the laws of the State of Florida?"

"No, I guess not," he said sullenly.

I returned to the table where Ben had another folder ready. I carried it over to the witness. "You're the one who identified Frances' body, aren't you?"

"Yes." The bastard managed to croak out a tear on this one.

"And you told the authorities you were her father, right?"

"I *am* her father." He raised his voice slightly. "What are you trying to prove here?"

"So, your name was listed as the father on her death certificate."

"Of course, it was."

"Frances' date of birth was November 18, 2002, correct?"

I pulled an official looking document from the folder which clearly contained an embossed seal. He looked at it suspiciously. I could tell he thought it was her death certificate, which contained her date of birth.

"I think that's what it was."

"Frances' middle name was Patricia, correct?"

"Yeah."

"And Betty's last name is really Wilkinson, isn't it?"

"She's always used my name, but yes."

"I have here what appears to be an official birth certificate of a Frances P. Wilkinson, DOB 11/18/2002. It lists the mother as Betty Wilkinson."

I shoved it in front of his face. "Please read the name of Frances' father."

He wouldn't look at it, nor would he answer my question. I placed the tip of my finger on a box at the top left of the document. "Doesn't that say that Frances' father was Norman D. Yates, of San Bernardino, California?"

Dan loudly objected again, but Thorpe said, "I'm beginning to think this is all *very* relevant. The objection is overruled."

"Mr. Lathrop, do you need me to call Mrs. Betty Wilkinson, who's sitting directly behind our counsel table, to come up here right now and swear to this jury that you are in fact not the father of Frances Wilkinson, as you've always maintained?"

Again, no answer.

"Your Honor, I offer into evidence this certified copy of the birth certificate of Frances P. Wilkinson."

Thorpe didn't wait to see if there was an objection from Dan and said, "Mr. Clerk, it may be admitted as Defense Exhibit Twenty." He then turned back toward Jerry Lathrop. "Mr. Lathrop, I must caution you that perjury in my court, or any other court, is a felony in the State of Florida."

Jerry didn't look up. His head hung down to his mid-chest. Frankly, I had him right where I wanted him.

"Mr. Lathrop, did you hear what I said?" Thorpe repeated.

"Yes, judge," Lathrop whispered.

"You may continue, Mr. Harris."

I went back and retrieved Lieutenant Milbury's report from Ben, who was ready with it.

"Mr. Lathrop, were you aware that Betty Wilkinson, and I now choose to call her by her legal name, told Lieutenant Milbury of the Monroe County Sheriff's Office . . ." and I read verbatim from the report.

"That's a fucking lie. All of it," he said.

"Mr. Lathrop, you are one profanity away from being held in summary contempt of this court," Thorpe told him.

I said, "In fact, Mr. Lathrop, Betty Wilkinson testified, in addition to this report, that your shoes were wet after you came home from searching for Frances. Did you know that?"

"More goddamn . . . more lies."

I walked directly up to Lathrop, my face no more than a foot from his. "In fact, Mr. Lathrop, you were caught in your home having sex with your friend Stearn, an officer with the Key West Police Department, by your daughter on the afternoon of June 14. You strangled her, you both raped and sodomized her, and abandoned and bludgeoned her body at the Salt Ponds. In fact, I bet the unknown donor DNA on the murder weapon will be Stearn's, won't it, Jerry Lathrop?"

I noticed him duck down and make a quick movement toward his ankle. I instinctively stepped back a stride. The first thing I observed when he came up was the same venomous look on his face, the one I had seen when he came into my house many months ago. The second was the strangest looking instrument I had ever seen. It was in his right hand. It was compact and yellowish in color. I didn't realize it was a gun until a bright orange flash jumped out of its end and I felt a searing pain on the left side of my head. I twisted around and as I did I saw Bob's head kick back, and when it snapped forward again, I observed a perfect round hole in the center of his forehead.

I remember, and it was only a nanosecond, bracing for the next bullet to slam into my body. It didn't, only because when Bob slumped down in his chair, I could see Betty behind him, now standing, holding a similar looking object in her hand. It gave out the same flash. I turned toward where it was pointing, and saw Jerry Lathrop's left eye disappear in an explosion of juices and colors. His body shuddered for a moment, then slid lazily down off the witness chair.

Chapter Forty

An eerie silence descended upon the courtroom. I found myself sitting on the floor directly in front of the witness box. The only sound was an increasing ringing in my ears, as if someone were striking a Tibetan bell inside my cranium. I looked around and from my low vantage-point could only see Ben and Betty Lathrop standing. Ben was leaning over Bob, dabbing hopelessly at the hole in his head with his handkerchief. Betty approached me, then crouched and held a handful of tissues against the side of my head. I saw blood . . . a lot of it.

Then the room sprang to life. A bevy of court officers blasted through the main door. I saw jurors and some spectators tentatively rise up in their seats. Judge Thorpe called for order, but I detected a tremor in his otherwise strong voice. The jury was quickly led out, and EMT's entered shortly after the officers. I was bundled up onto a gurney and transported, sirens blazing, to the Lower Keys Medical Center.

Ben and Janine arrived within minutes. They were allowed to stay while the nurses cleaned up around my ear. They all agreed I was extremely fortunate—the bullet had just grazed my head, lopping off a good piece of my ear in the process.

"Ben, could you tell what shape Bob was in?" I asked.

"He's dead, Sam. No doubt about it. And Lathrop as well."

"Jesus Christ. Anyone else hurt?"

"Miraculously, no."

Janine came over and buried her head next to mine in the pillow—on my non-injured side, that is. "Babe, are you going to be okay?"

"So long as you can still be in love with a one-eared man."

"They'll fix that up in no time, you just wait and see."

Epilogue

I dislike epilogues. Especially in novels. Life is not that easily summarized and structured.

But I must add one here. As with the trial, I was forced to suffer too many uncertainties not to try to bring some order to them. Where to start? With me, of course. Plastic surgery produced a reasonable facsimile of my wounded ear. I just wore my hair longer to cover the unavoidable scar tissue.

Stearn was scientifically tied to the DNA on the stick of wood. Jerry Lathrop, to my great chagrin, received a police honor guard send-off at the cemetery. The Key West Citizen published a police publicity snippet that suggested I had driven "the oft-honored Officer Lathrop" to the precipice, which resulted in his shooting Bob and me.

Bob was handled more traditionally. All his bocce brothers—and drinking buddies—raised sufficient funds to cremate him and blast his ashes into the ozone via a rented miniature cannon off of Fort Zachary Taylor Park.

Betty was not charged, clearly acting in the defense of others. A possible charge of possessing an illegal firearm—it turned out to be a high-tech carbon .22, two-shot derringer, one of a set of two that belonged to Jerry—was silently swept under the carpet. She left Key West very shortly after the trial to parts unknown.

Janine and I were married a month after. Somehow the danger and trauma we underwent pulled us together in a way normal existence never could. We now wake up in the same bed every morning.

Alice returned to San Francisco, but we talk a few times a week, and we plan a trip out there, and she to Key West, at least once a year.

What did I do? I quit the practice of law, got my captain's license, and am now piloting one of the catamarans that plies the warm waters around Key West with reveling tourists. No stress, no-brainer, and keeps me well away from the land-based gendarmes who still somehow blame me for Jerry Lathrop's death.

Why didn't I just pull up stakes and leave Key West once and for all? Because I love this place, even with its craziness, its subculture of graft and greed. Just go out on the gin-clear waters; cruise the backcountry; spend an afternoon on an isolated sandbar adjacent to a mangrove island. You'll see what I mean. I hope to die here—later not sooner.

CAST OF CHARACTERS

(In order of their appearance)

Chapter One

1) Bob Wilson
2) Harley, Bob's Rottweiler/Doberman mix dog
3) Jessica, Sam's Collie and Shepherd mix
4) Sam Harris

Chapter Two

5) Janine Williams, aka Reynolds
6) Detective Kenneth Phillips
7) Detective Robert Albury
8) Frances Lathrop
9) Judge Jeremiah Thorpe
10) Dan Thompson, prosecutor

Chapter Three

11) Officer Reynolds
12) Officer Murphy
13) Lisa Mahoney, placed 911 call to police
14) Charlie, the bartender
15) Chief Fitzpatrick

Chapter Four

16) Dr. Manish Agawar, performed the autopsy on Frances

17) Victoria White, assistant to Dr. Agawar

18) Jerry Lathrop

Chapter Five

19) Peter Warren

20) Sally Berkshire

Chapter Six

21) Dr. Henry Gordon, DNA expert

Chapter Seven

22) Donna Williams, office landlord's wife

23) Ralph DePiero

Chapter Eight

24) Officer Carney, friend of Ralph DePiero's who let him near the crime scene

Chapter Nine

25) Officer Stearn

26) Cheri, the gate keeper at Dan's office

Chapter Ten

27) Cody Thurston, guy who looks at Bob's phone

Chapter Eleven

28) Steve and Roseanne Jones

29) Michael (Jerry's brother, whose ID he has taken over)

Chapter Twelve

30) Tyler, the guy who worked on the photos

Chapter Thirteen

31) Emmanuel Gonzales

32) Charon Gonzales

Chapter Fourteen

33) Scotty (deceased child of Trudy Collins)

34) Trudy Collins, mother of Scotty, accused of killing her son and suffering from Munchhausen by proxy syndrome

35) Ed Warren, attorney for the Florida Childrens Protective Agency

Chapter Sixteen

36) Tim Hoffman, the local attorney who tells Sam the headless torso is Manny.

7) Officer Peters (the Florida State Investigator who accosts Sam at Manny's funeral)

Chapter Nineteen

38) Lt. Milbury (interviewed Betty Lathrop)

39) Betty Lathrop

40) Stephen Baxter (the snitch)

41) Sheriff Randall (who first met with the snitch)

42) Carl Atkins, the State Police fingerprint expert.

Chapter Twenty

43) Benjamin Schultz

44) Charles Knowles, Key West scion, whose estate plan Ben had done

Chapter Twenty-One

45) Reynolds (Janine's prior married name)

46) Lady Divine; Sister Boom-Boom; Hedda Lettuce; Salvatore Graziano (Sally's former stage names, and her real name)

Chapter Twenty-Three

47) Mary, Sam's sister

Chapter Twenty-Four

48) Alice, Janine's mother

49) Officer Shields (cop Sam thinks he saw in San Fran)

Chapter Twenty-Six

50) Sullivan, aka Sully (the prison guard who let the inmates into PC to hurt Bob)

Chapter Thirty

51) Bridget, Dan's young assistant

Chapter Thirty-One

52) Robert Hutchins, the Corrections Officer who overheard Bob say he was guilty

Chapter Thirty-Four

53) Dr. Carlos Attila

Made in the USA
Columbia, SC
14 December 2018